D1331226

SELF-CONTROL

OTHER WORKS BY STIG SÆTERBAKKEN IN
ENGLISH TRANSLATION

Siamese

SELF-CONTROL

STIG SÆTERBAKKEN

Translated by Seán Kinsella

DALKEY ARCHIVE PRESS

CHAMPAIGN • DUBLIN • LONDON

Originally published in Norwegian as *Selvbeherskelse* by J.W. Cappelen, Oslo, 1998

Library of Congress Cataloging-in-Publication Data

Sæterbakken, Stig, 1966-2012.
[Selvbeherskelse. English]
Self-control / Stig S3/4terbakken ; translated by Sean Kinsella. -- 1st ed.
     p. cm.
"Originally published in Norwegian as Selvbeherskelse by J.W. Cappelen, Oslo, 1998."
   ISBN 978-1-56478-813-9 (pbk. : alk. paper) -- ISBN 978-1-56478-785-9 (cloth : alk. paper)
 1. Paralytics--Fiction. 2. Family--Fiction. 3. Married people--Fiction. 4. Husbands--Fiction. I. Kinsella, Seán. II. Title.
 PT8951.29.A39S4513 2012
 839.82'374--dc23
                              2012020820

Partially funded by the Norwegian Ministry of Foreign Affairs, and by a grant from the Illinois Arts Council, a state agency.

This translation has been published with the financial support of NORLA.

Supported using public funding by the National Lottery through Arts Council England.

NORWEGIAN MINISTRY OF FOREIGN AFFAIRS

Illinois ARTS Council

LOTTERY FUNDED

Supported using public funding by
ARTS COUNCIL ENGLAND

www.dalkeyarchive.com

Cover: design and composition by Mikhail Iliatov

Printed on permanent/durable acid-free paper and bound in the United States of America

SELF-CONTROL

I hadn't seen her . . . talked to her of course, but hadn't seen her, in . . . how many years had it been? . . . even though she was my own flesh and blood . . . and that's why it seemed natural to me to explain it this way, because it was as though the opportunity arose so seldom that it gave us both . . . or me at least . . . a sort of fear of failure with regard to the benefits of our rather hastily arranged meeting. Even though she wasn't the daughter who lived farthest away, no, on the contrary our homes were so close to each other that actually it was a wonder that we didn't bump into each other unexpectedly from time to time. That this wasn't the case made it natural to assume that it was because she didn't want to, and for that reason had taken measures not to . . . or simply . . . and perhaps more likely . . . because it was extremely seldom that I . . . if at all in the past year . . . had deviated from my regular daily route through the city.

She had lit a long, thin cigarillo, I got the idea that it was chosen on account of her fingers, which were also very long and thin. She kept looking out the window all the time, as if there was something exciting going on out there, or she stared down at the table or at the cigarillo when I answered her or asked about something: surveying with great interest, it seemed, the grey glow advancing down along the slim stem. A bit put-on, this excessive nonchalance. But what else could I expect? Every time she opened her mouth I thought I'd hear something terrible, that she'd blame me for something, or tell me about something horrible that had happened to her. But after a while, as the conversation ran its course, still without any particularly unpleasant subjects being brought up, I ascertained to my surprise that it was all progressing in an extremely polite and restrained way: I couldn't help but imagine how friendly and relaxed our little meeting would appear to an outsider, one of the café's random patrons.

I took a glance out the window, in the hope of perhaps discovering something of interest that could explain her slight absentmindedness. But there was nothing to see, not from where I was sitting anyway, nothing other than a fire hydrant that stood on the other side of the street, squeezed against the fence, with a drooping bush as a roof. It had a sort of dignity, standing there. A few long blades of grass had struggled up through the asphalt and grown closely around it, and a couple of dandelions had accompanied them, of which there were only a few greenish-brown leaves left, making it look like a headstone. It was completely calm, cars passed without a sound. Yes, it all seemed so peaceful that it appeared almost staged. I started to think about that girl who'd been reported missing earlier in the day, she was sixteen and hadn't come home from a party the night before. We'd heard the police appeals on the news during our lunch break but it didn't seem like anyone else had taken any particular notice of it . . . perhaps you just hear about that sort of thing too often nowadays? . . . and this had exasperated me, I realized, even though it was only now, in retrospect, that I noticed what an impression it had made. It was so tranquil in the park as well, when I strolled through it, a bit before six, and still warm in the sunlight. The pea shrub bushes crackled like a lively fire in a hearth along the promenade, the empty pods hitting the asphalt with a dry slap. She'd suggested the place to meet, I had to ask for directions twice. And when I finally opened the door, a couple of minutes late, and caught sight of her . . . she had sat down at a round table, in the middle of the café . . . there was something strange about her, just at first glance, that made me proud, like a confirmation of something, without my being sure of what it was.

Our chairs were plastic, the seat felt cold against my behind when I sat down and I had a hard time ignoring the goose bumps it gave me on my skin down there, it felt like tiny nails being pulled out of my rear. All at once I became aware that I was frightened of running out of things to say, and I thought I recognised the same fear in her. Then I thought that I could actually say anything at all, that it still wouldn't make any difference. It was as though the lack of contact, on a regular basis, which at some times bothered me and at other times didn't, relieved us of all responsibility: however you looked at it, we didn't have the time we'd need to become so acquainted with one another that it would be of any significance, no matter what we said. At the same time I couldn't quite get away from feeling a certain sort of secret admiration for her. Because I did see, to my amazement, that it was a grown-up and extremely sensible woman sitting in front of me, one who wouldn't allow herself be knocked off her perch just like that, wonderful to see, yes, quite beautiful actually, it struck me, as I studied her more closely. I thought I could picture her reprimanding one of her colleagues for substandard work, or rolling her eyes over a particularly stupid remark from Karl-Martin, with whom she had unfortunately and for reasons that were incomprehensible ended up with; she who could probably have chosen anyone she wanted . . .

"You're all settled in then?" I asked.

"Yeah," she answered, a little sullenly, as if the question bored her.

"And everything at work is all right?"

"Yeah."

"And Karl-Martin?"

"Karl-Martin's work is okay too. He's just started in a new job. The last job he had was just awful, he hated it so much he was on the verge of . . . well."

I nodded, even though I didn't know what she was going to say.

"But he's happy now," she said, it seemed like fatigue was on the verge of overwhelming her.

"Do the two of you have any particular plans, or . . ."

I immediately regretted the unfinished sentence, because I knew she wouldn't help me in the way I had helped her. She looked at me. As I'd thought. She just waited.

"Or are you both . . . ?" I felt I'd already entangled myself in something that would be impossible to find my way out of again.

"Y'know? Thinking, right now, how should I put it . . . ?"

She gave a wry grin. "About children, you mean?"

I threw my hands up. "Yes, for example."

"That can wait," she said, but it seemed from the way she said it as though this was out of the question. She began to tell me about Karl-Martin's job, not her own . . . described in detail what his new position involved, how much responsibility he'd been given, how much they expected of him, how much freedom he had to plan his workdays.

While I sat there listening to her I noticed something peculiar about her lips, how they stuck to each other at a particular point at the far corner of one side of her mouth when she spoke. This detail, insignificant as it was, now caught my attention in such a way that I lost sight of everything else. I couldn't manage to take my eyes off it. It bothered me to look at it, all the same I let myself become completely absorbed by it. There was something about it that didn't fit . . . was that why I was so fascinated? . . . the rest of her, something that didn't match, no, absolutely not, with what I otherwise took as being her, or rather her outward face. It was as though that small, and to a certain extent innocent, defect did something to her expression, gave her a certain quality of . . . well, mercilessness, completely lacking in compassion, as if she was ready to clear every obstacle out of her way by whatever means necessary. It frightened me when I saw it. *It was like I was sitting face to face with a superior power.* I looked at her, closely examined her whole face, which I had studied with pleasure only a few minutes before . . . but it seemed as though it had changed, and now I thought it was a wonder that I hadn't noticed it right away, this cool, calculating, yes, *cynical* feature of her mouth. It wasn't possible not to see it. And what I had initially considered a disruptive element, a blemish, was now revealed as the very thing that, in reality, gave her her own particular appearance. I stared at her mouth: unmistakeably hers. And eventually . . . unavoidably perhaps . . . there was something nasty about it, the slow, sort of lazy motion at the corner of her mouth . . . it was as though I was hearing the sound of them, her lips, every time they tore free of one another, again and again, for every word she spoke. And it was only when I realized that she had been sitting staring at me a while without saying anything that I managed to tear my eyes away from that fold of skin . . . only to discover that I hadn't the slightest notion of anything appropriate to say . . .

Once again it was she who saved us from an embarrassing silence.

"How are things with Mom anyway?" she asked, in an offhand kind of way, as if it didn't matter to her whether she got a proper answer or not.

"Marit," I said, squeezing my buttocks together, because a brief bout of stomachache had suddenly become a bubble of air that wanted to get out, and it was as if the coldness of the seat was trying to pull it out of me by force.

"Your mother and I, we're getting a divorce."

She was startled. It was as unexpected for her as it was for me. I had to use all my strength to tame the demon that was wreaking havoc down in my rear end, a loud piercing fart cracked against the seat before I managed to gag it, but she was, fortunately, too beside herself to notice. Because we both sat there, shocked by what we had heard. Yes, even she sat there now, with glistening eyes and a flushing flower on each cheek. But only for a moment, she was quick to regain her composure, find her way back to her pale, feigned attitude of insensitivity.

"I see," she said. "I see, so the two of you are getting a divorce."

A few moments passed, then she added: "That was a surprise." She shrugged, in resignation . . . or indifference perhaps . . . as if to illustrate how little she cared, and drank what looked like the last dregs from her cup. I said a silent prayer that she would let the subject lie, which it seemed she wanted to do as well. She was probably uneasy about showing too much interest in the unexpected news, and at that moment I was indebted to her for exactly that. Because what would I have answered, if she had begun to question me . . . about the cause of the breakup . . . about our reasons for wanting to leave each other . . . about how we planned to organize our new lives . . . when we had no intention at all of doing any of it?

My spontaneous lie made it difficult for us to continue our conversation, that was plain to see. So I drank up as well, a cold, pasty sediment that made me shiver, and we took care of what we had met up to take care of in the twinkling of an eye, quickly and efficiently, without saying any more than was necessary to each other, like a customer and an employee; I gave her the money, we exchanged a few words, I waved to the waiter and asked for the bill. Marit insisted on paying, but I was strongly opposed, there was no sense in it, I thought, if she was going to use the money she had just gotten.

She said good-bye to me as soon as we were outside the café. I was a little bewildered since the most natural thing would have been for me to accompany her, I could almost have followed her home without going out of my way . . . on the other hand I was also aware of how easily an awkward atmosphere could develop in the course of an unplanned extension of our time together . . . possibly it was precisely this that she was considerate enough to want to avoid by our taking leave of each other . . . or she could have to run an errand downtown for that matter . . . what did I know? I wondered if I should ask her to say hello to Karl-Martin, but thought it best not to mention his name any more than was absolutely necessary. We shook hands. And suddenly I felt the impulse to hug her, to hold her, just for a moment . . . be left with a perfumed imprint on my body as a memento . . . but I refrained, I thought that it would only make the situation more difficult for her. And for me. Maybe she would have to twist herself free from the embrace . . . *as from an assault* . . . and then she would have gone home with the feeling that she'd been molested, a feeling which would then be imprinted on her memory of this meeting, overshadowing all its positive aspects, no matter if they were in the majority . . . *which they were* . . . as opposed to now, I thought as I stood there watching her walk away, there where we parted, if not in an especially affectionate way, then at least in a polite and level-headed one, so she could walk home, if not with any great happiness, that's for sure, then without bearing a grudge, without having experienced her father as a particularly clumsy or unpleasant person.

Her head stuck up out of the coat like a flower from a vase, I saw her neck, white beneath her close-cropped hair, and I thought I could almost picture the way it had been when she was small . . . there was something about her neck . . . their necks . . . that made such an impression on me every time I saw them, although I couldn't remember the reason. But there was something nervous about the way she walked, out here . . . she sort of danced along . . . which didn't quite fit with the impression I had gotten from her in there, cool and self-assured, *that arrogant attitude* she had adopted . . . which she had probably had from the start, it had just

taken a little time before I recognised it . . . and which my insane
fabrication about the divorce had been the only thing that . . . for
a fraction of a second . . . had managed to puncture. I tried to
remember if I'd had any firm opinion of myself when I was her
age. In any case, I was convinced it was a lot less developed and
self-assured than hers. I had once wished all the best for her, I
thought, no matter what. As little pain as possible, and as much
joy as possible. That she would succeed in everything she did,
however far her interests might be from the pursuits I myself considered meaningful. No matter what she chose to invest her time
and energy in, that the investment would prove to be worthwhile,
that the profit would be plentiful, that her efforts would only make
her stronger. I wanted her to be a fast learner, wanted her to do all
right as far as her circles of friends; wanted her to have, preferably,
a prominent position; wanted her not to be bothered by anyone,
have the wool pulled over her eyes by anyone; not to be exploited
by any two-faced creeps, stripped of her independence and self-
respect by some twisted psychopath or other. I wondered if she
and Nina still kept in touch, or if the years had come between
them, as they can so easily, and so quickly, between siblings . . . and
I remembered that that was what I'd been thinking about beforehand and had wanted to ask her, if it had been a long time since
she'd heard anything from Nina, if they ever met up, or rang each
other now and again, if she knew where Nina was at the moment,
where she lived, who she lived with if she wasn't living alone . . . I
tried to think, were they more alike than unlike, those two, would
a stranger seeing them for the first time notice the similarities or
the differences if told that they were sisters. But it was as though

I couldn't quite manage to picture both of them side by side . . . it was as though I didn't have room in my thoughts for the both of them . . . only Marit, or someone who resembled Marit . . .

She disappeared behind a growling bus, and I couldn't help feeling a certain relief at the thought that it would probably be a good while before we would meet again. I let my eyes wander, slowly. I tried to remember if there was any particular name for them, the clouds I saw, which looked like they were stuck to the blue of the sky, clouds that would soon diminish and which awoke a strange and highly conflicted feeling in me . . . *It was as though I was close to exploding with joy over something that in reality was dreadfully sad.* I stood looking at the traffic light, just there where Marit had disappeared, a round, red blot, like an overripe apple that would soon fall. Finally I decided to go . . . why hang around there, in the middle of a busy sidewalk, with my bag in my hand? . . . besides, I was freezing . . . and I turned my head slowly as I walked so as not to let the traffic light out of my sight: I thought that if it changes to green while I can still see it then a disaster is going to take place somewhere in the world tonight, a catastrophe so big that it would be all over the front pages tomorrow morning and that there'd be newsflashes on the television all afternoon . . . several hundred people dead, an entire area razed to the ground . . . but nothing happened, it was still red as I crossed the street and went into the parking lot outside the big shopping centre on the other side: its name stood humming in the twilight in a seething shimmer of orange and yellow. My hands turned yellow, and the people I met looked sinister, as if their faces were about to come loose from their bodies. Even the parked cars shone in the light of the store's letters, like animals asleep in a field.

More agitated than usual . . . yes . . . I put the key into old man Schiong's pride and joy, a shining wrought-iron gate from before the First World War, given a new coat of paint every five years up until Didriksen came and took over . . . dried flakes peeling back like bits of black paper in a wreath around the big keyhole, I can hardly bear to think of it. But the familiar dusty and dry atmosphere inside soon calmed me down . . . helped me slowly but surely regain my composure. That, and the distinctive tightness of the hairnet around my head, which was like the beginning of a vague headache. There was something so blissfully imperturbable about this big room with all its machines, which I was the first to enter as usual while bit by bit it flickered and fell into place under the light of the fluorescent tubes in the ceiling. Everything was just as it had always been. And in this calm, this majestic steadfastness, I walked around and flipped the switches, like an ancient, millennial ritual, and the deep rumbling of the machines filled me with that sensation of pleasure and peace which every morning makes me feel I belong to a world over which I am in complete control, similar to what it must be like to finally get indoors . . . I imagine that's what it must be like, anyway . . . after being out in a fierce storm for hours.

One minor problem. A machine, number four, stopped at lunchtime, after having given us a brief warning in the form of a sweet, black puff of smoke from its valve . . . like a reminder of the times they ran on paraffin . . . only to fall silent soon after, as if someone had turned it off. The boss soon appeared. From force of habit he turned to me to find out what was going on, although strictly speaking number four wasn't my responsibility. Two of my colleagues had already unfastened the cover and stood shining flashlights inside it. I explained to the boss, as far as I could surmise, where the fault in all likelihood was to be found, what could possibly have caused it, and in what way and how fast, if need be, we could repair it. He listened to what I had to say with a few sullen grunts, and then looked briefly around the inside of the machine as if to verify what I'd said, even though I knew only too well, as did my colleagues, that he hadn't the faintest idea about the workings of the machines he owned, and that for him to stand studying the motor on a Hold-Martinsen 34 was akin to someone from the Middle Ages being presented with a Picasso. Then he stared at me again, with an angry look, as if he wanted to tone down his helplessness by demonstrating that he wasn't quite sure if he trusted my professional opinion. *He, who is completely at the mercy of these assessments.* His lips had sunk back into his mouth and didn't come out again, even when he spoke. Then he put a paternal hand on my shoulder and nodded approvingly before he shuffled off and crept up once more into that rat's nest of an office he has, half a story over the workshop floor, with its tinted window . . . *the embrasure* as we call it . . . where he can see us, but we can't see him.

Jens-Olav, who'd had his head stuck down inside the machine for almost a quarter of an hour, turned and peered at me with those little slitty eyes of his, as if he wanted to draw my attention to some oversight. I don't know if it was to get away from that accusatory look . . . *and I've asked myself several times if it feels accusatory because it's justified?* . . . but anyway I did something that I usually only do when the situation is so serious that it's demanded of me: I walked over to the boss's office and knocked on the door. I regretted it immediately, because going in there was, as always, awkward. The exterior door to the office was down on our level, so that after you'd gotten your "come in" and had opened it, you still had the stairs left to climb: the first thing you saw was the boss's head, high above, like that of a sweaty little god, hovering on a cloud of solid wood, which in reality is an ordinary desk, but which seems enormous when seen from underneath. And as you ascend the three or four steps . . . aren't they unusually high as well? It feels like that, anyway . . . he, the boss, has ample time to study the person approaching him.

I took off my hairnet the way you'd doff your hat to the lord of the manor. The company's only computer was on the desk in front of him, in the one place where it was probably of least use. There was a bowl of honey on top of it, which he used to lure flies. The window overlooking the street was kept open all summer long and ensured a constant supply of the species . . . they were everywhere . . . and it didn't make any difference if the window was closed because the flies still kept on pouring out of their snug hiding places in cracks and ventilators and everywhere in the gaps in the moulding, they obviously settle in there, legions of them, in the walls and floors and behind the wallpaper, and continue to breed as long as the warmth keeps them alive. Enticed by the heavy sweetness from the honey bowl, or by the lure of the skirting boards, candy red against the white of the walls, they head out and lose their way in the open . . . a short, intense flight . . . until the swatter catches up with them and mashes their quivering happiness into a shapeless yellow pulp. He always gets them. He never misses. He says he can *feel* it. He *knows* when the time is right and he can strike with everything he's got.

The boss pointed something out to me once, the fact that it's impossible to kill a fly with a single blow, no matter how hard you hit or how accurate you are. Maybe it's because of the mesh in the swatter, which is there to reduce drag . . . another thing I'd never considered until he mentioned it . . . and which always leaves a small part of the insect unscathed? All you're doing is knocking them unconscious. Even when they're badly messed up, even when the white vestiges of life are oozing out of them as a more than demonstrable sign of their defeat, it's still, according to the boss, just a matter of time until they come back to life. He's told me how he's seen some of them dragging themselves across the desk, just barely intact, the tiniest remainder, but alive just the same . . . like a buzzing mote moving across the table top, as he so vividly described it. You have to go further if you want to get rid of them for good. He's explained it all to me and shown me how he does it. On the small display table, with the coffee and the kettle on top, he keeps a plastic bag: with his hand inside it, so he avoids touching them, he picks up the unconscious fly and crushes it between his fingers, and then, as a last precaution, he drops the remains into a glass preserve jar, where there are already thousands of earlier victims, and screws the top on tight over the mass grave.

I've never seen him empty it, not once in all these years has the stock diminished . . . maybe his goal isn't to rid the office of them but to fill up his jar?

Now that I'd disturbed him . . . while he was in the middle of something utterly unimportant, no doubt, and without any particular goal in mind, I just stood there . . . my mouth slightly open perhaps . . . in front of the desk, probably looking confused and indecisive . . . as indeed I was. Besides that, the smell of the honey was making me dizzy. Maybe that's why he keeps the bowl there, I thought, not to attract the flies but to anaesthetise his visitors, all of whom without exception he regards as his enemies, to knock them off balance before they have a chance to cross the starting line. What was I going to say? What impulse had brought me up here? And then it was as though I had only now realized how unreasonable this situation was, the entirely random and extreme absurdity of the fact that he, this little rodent, should be sitting there as my superior, and I, Andreas Felt, should be standing there with my cap in my hand bowing and scraping for what little he might spare me. Was this pathetic figure sitting there, *five to ten years my junior,* really the person to whom, according to the rules, I was obliged to defer? To be at his beck and call, to cater to his every whim, whatever it might be at any given time, every single day from early morning until the working day was done? It made me furious now that I thought about it. This anaemic huckster, this pallid character who had *brownnosed* his way to the top and hadn't lifted a finger since, just sat idly for hours on end in an overheated office in front of a computer he barely knew how to turn on and off . . . What real power did he have over me, when it came down to it? On the contrary, wasn't it closer to the truth that the power relationship between us was so fragile, so completely removed from reality, constructed upon formalities and nothing else, *absolutely nothing else*, that we only needed to leave the premises and go to another place up the street, to Mehrum's Bakery, in order to see how ludicrous it was, how implausible it was, how downright *embarrassing* it was, and how it would dissolve irretrievably and turn to dust as soon as a different and slightly fresher air was let in?

"Get up, you little shit," I said to him, which was as good a thing to say as any after such a long pause, which looked like it was about to drive him over the edge in any case, unaccustomed as he was, no doubt, to being faced with silence when someone had taken the trouble to come see him. It was hard to say whether he was relieved or appalled that the silence was now being broken. He sat there stooped and sullen in any case, motionless, with his little gimlet eyes that he couldn't manage to keep still. I saw that he was missing a button on his shirt, that it was his tie which was keeping his collar in place, and this inspired me to go that much further.

"Get up and listen to what I've got to say!" I said, overconfidence making me pompous and bombastic. Because he really was a pathetic sight, sitting there pale as if he'd just been to the doctor and received a death sentence by way of a merciless x-ray. There was nothing else for it but to let rip, something I felt duty bound to commit to anyway, now that I'd started.

"You little shit!" I roared at him, "hiding away so that people can't see just how ridiculous and incompetent you actually are! Sitting rotting in an office all day long. Your name might be on that brass plate outside the door but you're not the boss. You probably couldn't put two words together if someone came up and asked you what it is we actually do here! Why? Because all you know how to do is cheat! All you've learned to do in life is to sneak, and swindle, and suck up! All you're good for is lying and deceiving! There's nothing more pathetic than the sort of people who cheat because they can't succeed any other way! Shrewd and spineless, what a wonderful combination! But every fraud in the world has more dignity than you! You asshole! You're the sort who cheats his parents from the time he's born, who dupes and deceives his friends, who'd have cheated on his girlfriends if he had any, and whose crowning glory, after years of swindling, was his wedding day! All you've ever earned money on was deceit! Everything you've built up and all the times you've succeeded, all of it was a swindle from start to finish, you miserable bastard!"

Fired up by my own words, and with an intense pressure in my chest from the excitement, I leaned over his desk and roared, more at the shiny forehead than at the man slumped under it: "I've seen your notes on the desk drawer, so I know how you think! I know how you work! If you can call it working, earning money the same way you wring out a cloth! I know how you've got a hold over the old man! I know all about your methods, how you began to ingratiate yourself when the time was ripe, how you stayed in the background and let everyone else have their say, and then afterward you took Schiong aside and told him what *you* thought! How you found out about the unpaid bills, and about the health insurance, which were only mere formalities, problems that could be fixed in a wink, and how you blew them up out of all proportion to Schiong, who was long past understanding anything like that, and how you talked him into letting you take care of it, quietly, and how in reality you didn't need to do anything at all apart from make a few calls and reallocate some insignificant funds! How you patted him on the shoulder afterward and told him he could relax now, that everything had been taken care of, that everything was in safe hands! *Safe Hands!* The greediest, filthiest, most unscrupulous sticky-fingered pair of crook's hands known to man!"

All the yelling had begun to take it out of me. I took a breath and leaned back but not so far that I didn't keep a good grip with both hands on the edge of the desk. Before I continued, I lowered my voice, a murderous whisper accompanied by an almost inaudible whistling: "A good few of your workers are starting to get on in years, you realize that? Some of them might retire as early as next year. What are you going to do then? Where do you plan on finding the new blood to replace the old guys down there? How do you plan on replacing your workforce, something that *has* to happen, and still manage to come close to maintaining current levels of production? Do you think kids today have the least bit of interest or respect for a business as unprofitable as this? They want to step out into the light, not down into the darkness and noise of this place. Do you think that on the day we all leave you there'll be nine fresh-faced kids standing down there, in our workshop coats, one machine each, blessed with the knowledge and patience we have, to guarantee that this lousy little business of yours, in spite of old and out-dated equipment, doesn't suffer in the least as far as efficiency and delivery schedule? And what about the technological revolution that's set to explode all through trade and industry, have you considered that? Have you any idea at all of what demands are going to be made? Have you, and I just thought of this now, have you any concept at all of what *quality* means? Or maybe you just think it's a matter of getting hold of some people who work *fast enough?* You should consider yourself lucky, you crook, that the business you got your hands on almost runs itself. You should thank the devil that it was all in place, the whole thing, the day you made a fool of old Schiong. Because you, Konrad Didriksen, are one of the worst imaginable types of creep that crawls on the surface of the earth, living off of all the misery you manage to sniff out, and if something isn't already rotten the day you get your claws into it, then you make sure it perishes, you soil it and contaminate it so that it's ready to be taken over and the death blow can be dealt without your risking anything at all."

I remained standing when I had finished, and he stayed seated, and there wasn't a sound from him or from me, neither of us moved a muscle. I didn't quite know how I should feel after finally speaking my mind in that way . . . I noticed that I was sad more than anything, sad on both our behalfs, standing there in the unbearable heat from his electric radiators in the mistaken belief that it served any purpose. I got it into my head that it was up to me to break the spell. But I couldn't manage to say anything, so instead I cleared my throat: Didriksen gave a start, and then he stood up, as if he'd been asked to give a speech. With a contemptuous sneer, he made clear what he thought about what I'd said, as a pretext to come and disturb him while he was working, what an impudent *little idiot*, what a spineless bunch of *bastards* we all were . . . without meeting my eyes a single time, instead looking around continuously, as if trying to locate something in the room that could confirm his preposterous accusations. Fortunately he was standing with the fly-swatter in his hand and now he shook it, weakly, as if fanning himself in the stifling heat, while he told me what a *wretched person* he thought I was for disturbing him in the middle of his work for nothing . . . he wondered if I'd spared a thought about everything that was piling up down there in the meantime . . . if I had even considered the responsibility that rested with *him* at the end of the day . . . he repeated that last part a couple of times: rested with *him*, rested with *him* . . . and then he motioned angrily with his hand, with the result that he give himself a whack on the mouth with the swatter: at which point, finally, he looked up at me, as if he instinctively blamed me for this. I averted my eyes and caught sight of the white entrails of a fly hanging off the side of his computer . . . it looked like an abscess had been squeezed out of its grey skin . . . he'd obviously landed a direct hit right before I'd made my entrance. There was no way I could imagine that there was any chance at all of that thin lump regaining consciousness and yet it occurred to me that Didriksen was impatient to be left alone so that he could go over to get his bag and finish the job before it was too late.

But I was hardly halfway down the stairs when he started to speak again, and now in a voice that was barely recognisable.

"My wife is very ill," he said, as if he was talking to himself, but hoping that I'd overhear.

I remained standing with one foot poised over a step, unable to decide which reaction would be most natural. But soon I'd hesitated for so long that there was no going back. I turned and said: "Excuse me?" as if I hadn't heard what he'd said.

He stood looking at me gratefully, as far as I could make out over the edge of the desk.

"My wife is very ill," he repeated, looking down as if he was ashamed of it.

"What's wrong with her?" I asked politely.

"A rare form of cancer," he replied, my question seemed to have made it easier for him because he was looking down at me again. "One there's no treatment for. They've tried everything, but nothing works."

"Can't they operate?" I asked, and thought that I could make out the beginning of an endless series of questions I could ask if necessary, in order to keep the conversation going.

He shook his head.

"No one will say anything," he said, his voice sounding like it might crack. "No one will tell me anything. I ask and ask, every single day I'm there, but they just answer in general terms that it's impossible to know for sure, that it could be months, that it could be years. And the worst part of it is that I'm certain that they *do* know. That every one of them dealing with her there, that they know exactly how long she's got left. They've just agreed between themselves that me and Kristine are better off not knowing."

It gave me a start when he mentioned her name, I couldn't quite make myself believe that he had a woman by his side, this hairless flycatcher who paid me my wages every fortnight without fail.

"What do you think?" he continued. "What would you have done if you were me? Would you take them at their word when they say that they don't know? Or would you have pushed them until you squeezed the truth out of them?"

And when I didn't answer: "Which is better, do you think? To know the details, to know to the hour how long you have left, or not to know anything, as it would be otherwise, if there was no illness?"

I didn't know what to answer, and I wasn't really sure if he really wanted advice or if it was more important for him to present his problem to an outsider, someone he wasn't well acquainted with. I said it was something that it was difficult to have an opinion about before you found yourself in the same situation.

Didriksen nodded ponderously, as if he hadn't expected me to offer any particular opinion either. Then he looked at the clock.

"Well. They're probably waiting for you down there. But thank you. Thank you."

Slightly perplexed I went back to work, uncertain as to whether I'd now bolstered my position with the boss or emphatically destroyed what little standing I had managed to build up over the course of the last few years' unblemished record at such a small and easily surveyed workplace. The others glanced at me in passing, and these seemed more expressions of suspicion than any actual curiosity regarding my reasons for having a chat with the boss in his office and not even during break time. Kåre and Jens-Olav had managed to repair the damage while I'd been gone . . . the noise was back to full level . . . a polyphonic hum, a persistent booming drone as stolid as the surrounding walls, as solid and as durable as them in their delimitation of the room. Everyone had gotten back to what they were doing, an even ratio of men to machines, spread out over the large floor with approximately the same distance between them, like sculptures in a museum, and I thought, while I stood there . . . because that's one of the advantages of this type of work, that you don't need to think about it while you're doing it . . . that if it hadn't been for the racket we were making, if, on the contrary, all nine of us worked away in silence, busy with our own projects, then possibly the only sound we would have heard would have been the hollow blows against the wall from Mr Didriksen's office. I suppose that's the lot of insignificant people in life, they occupy themselves with insignificant things. That some of them still end up in important positions, in a roundabout way, is just the way it goes.

I glanced up at the large clock above the *embrasure*. Just a little after this time tomorrow Hans-Jacob and Elise would be paying their monthly visit. I don't know why I did it exactly . . . maybe in order to steel myself for what was coming . . . but I let the evening play out in my head just as I knew it would unfold . . . exactly as it would unfold . . . getting changed around six o' clock . . . Helene's imperious meal preparations . . . Her appeals for assistance, always with a hint of resentment, if there's something to be peeled or washed or chopped . . . The strange feeling I get walking around with shoes on indoors, as if I'm a stranger in my own home . . . The sound of the doorbell frightening me out of my wits because I've been walking around for the last hour waiting for it to ring . . . the slightly strained tone at the start, which we can never completely dispense with, no matter how well we all know each other . . . The conversation around the table that for a little while is intended to involve all four participants, but which soon divides into two, one between the men and one between the ladies . . .

Hans-Jacob always talks more than I do. He's the one who talks and I'm the one who responds. He's the one who brings things up

and I'm the one who chimes in. And sooner or later, come Saturday, Hans-Jacob will turn the conversation around to his favourite
subject, about a six-month course we both took a few years after
leaving school . . . at a time when we both had a lot of common interests and took for granted that we were going to work together . . .
and more specifically about a teacher we had in the course, who
had indeed been exceptionally talented. Moreover, he'd penned
several books within his particular field, which were the ones we'd
used when studying for the final exam, and which were also out of
the ordinary . . . so perhaps it's not so strange that Hans-Jacob is
always bringing the subject up, even though, like me, he probably
hasn't looked at the books since and so is relying on the memory of
his past enthusiasm. "That Vogt-Johannessen," he'll say, and draw
circles in the air with the end of his pipe, just as if we were sitting
in a café way back in the day, each with his beer, after our class was
over. And once more he'll talk about Vogt-Johannessen as if I didn't
know who he was, had never read him, and had no grasp at all of
the technical content of his work. But that's Hans-Jacob's way of
talking . . . as if the person listening doesn't have the faintest idea
what he's talking about. "That Vogt-Johannessen, Andreas . . . Vogt-
Johannessen . . ." He could continue like that the entire evening. In
which case his voice will gradually acquire more of a *singsong tone*
as he warms up to the subject. He'll gesticulate wildly and caress
his pipe as if it was a rare geological find . . . eventually it'll sound
like he's actually singing from his seat . . . casting resonant musical
waves that kind of *wash* or *throw* his conversational points over
the listener and make it impossible for me to question anything at
all. He never seems to go anywhere . . . not even to the traditional

Saturday dinner at our house, pleasant and relaxed as it's intended to be . . . without having thought out a list of topics beforehand that he can bring up and which he knows will arouse interest. On no occasion does he turn up unprepared. The worst thing about it is that he's usually studied the subjects so well that it's impossible to contradict him: all the facts are on his side.

I've never liked talking to him. And that's in spite of the fact that our conversations through the years probably amount to several thousand hours altogether. I don't know why. Perhaps it's because he's always so quick to respond, his answers so pertinent to what I ask him, even when he can't have guessed what I was going to bring up beforehand. It's annoying in the extreme. It's like he never lets me finish what I'm saying, as if there's some prestige for him in guessing the end of my sentence, preferably before I've gotten halfway. Still, it's nothing compared to what it was like when we were young, when we were seen as being joined at the hip, he was like a man possessed every time we bumped into someone: back then he used to speak just as often as he was able, even snatch the words out of my mouth if necessary. And on the rare occasions I managed to get a word in, he stared at me, terror-stricken while I spoke . . . sometimes he stood there stiff as a plank with his eyes wide, terrified in case I might say something interesting, something that would be worthy of note and remembered as a particularly astute or original remark. I'd imagine that's probably why Hans-Jacob has developed his own particular form of sarcasm over the years, in order to ensure that anything that I might come out with won't overshadow what he has said or is going to say. And on the rare occasions I did hit the nail on the head with

my, in Hans-Jacob's opinion, long-winded and humourless observations, then he was in there right away, almost before I had time
to draw breath, throwing in a thought uncannily like my own, but
formulated in his own characteristic way, as if raising up my ordinary and slightly boring utterance, making it into something bril-
liant, converting it into a deadly-accurate flick of the whip with
all the stinging irony he was so notorious for in our younger days,
as if to say to the rest of the group, please, excuse my friend here,
he doesn't know any better, but *this* is what he was actually trying
to say.

Back then I accepted it and viewed it as confirmation that he was
the more intelligent and enthusiastic of us two, always a head in
front of me, which I have to admit was true, many a time. But could
there have been other reasons behind it? Wasn't it likely . . . or *more*
likely, even . . . that it was *insecurity* that lay at the bottom of it, that
he was fairly insecure by nature and that this was why he'd gotten
into the habit of answering every question he was confronted with
so quickly and so pertinently . . . *simply in order to cover up the fact
that he was an extremely nervous person?* That it was something
he started doing because he was so terrified of not having an answer at hand, terrified of being at a loss for words, terrified of being caught out not knowing something? The thought delighted me.
Maybe, I thought, all these years I've been confusing *anxiety* with
wit, an anxiety Hans-Jacob has spent his whole life trying to hide?
Helene's always seemed pretty clear-sighted where it came to Elise
and Hans-Jacob, over the years. But she's never made the slightest
suggestion that Hans-Jacob is in reality quite a different character
than he pretends to be. She's normally so good at being able to see

through other people, read them like an open book . . . and suddenly it struck me . . . that Hans-Jacob's role as the dominant party in our relationship had possibly . . . or most likely . . . come about as much of a result of *importunity* and *obstinacy* on his part, more than any actual intelligence or sophistication. Yes, perhaps even to compensate for the *lack* of these qualities, I thought, which if he'd had them would have afforded him the natural, as opposed to the hard-earned, role of leader in our almost lifelong friendship. Maybe, in reality . . . and the thought gave me goose bumps as I went around from machine to machine with the greasing log, jotting down the tiny digits from the counters on each, decimals and all . . . that it is *I* who am superior to *him*, since I find it so easy to allow him take the lead . . . since I'm so willing to let him triumph . . . since it doesn't bother me much letting him outdo me, overwhelm me countless times in the course of a single evening when the four of us are together. And I couldn't get this thought out of my head . . . and couldn't help but ask myself . . . if this wasn't true superiority? . . . this calm certainty . . . this untapped potential . . . as opposed to Hans-Jacob's bluster and cheap triumphs? . . .

But these were things I didn't want to dwell on for too long, for fear of what I'd arrive at if I delved too deeply. I looked over the entries in the log . . . with feigned concentration . . . and compared them with last week's figures . . . but couldn't prevent my thoughts from following the trail they'd sighted. Could this be the reason I've always joked with Elise? I thought . . . always being slightly bold and rather inconsiderate toward her . . . maybe even bordering on offensive at times, for all I know? . . . with her it doesn't take much anyway . . . in order to keep my real feelings about her, and

Hans-Jacob too in fact, in check? Come to think of it, I've hardly exchanged a serious, let alone a sensible word with her. But there are certain people you have to joke with in order to endure being in their company. Elise is that kind of person. And by way of this jocularity I keep . . . in all likelihood perhaps have probably always kept . . . at arm's length . . . the fact that I really can't stand her.

Of course, Helene for her part misunderstands the whole thing. She's always perceived my little act with Elise . . . unavoidably perhaps . . . as *flirting* . . . albeit well within the bounds of decency . . . She still gets offended when she thinks I go too far. Then you just joke around with Hans-Jacob as much as I joke around with Elise, I was stupid enough to suggest in bed one night after they'd been to visit and we lay talking about the evening. Helene only needed to stick out her jaw and scratch her head like mad in order to get me to shut up and understand that I needn't repeat my suggestion. It was this parody that first drew my attention to the fact that Hans-Jacob has a slightly protruding jaw, something I'd never previously noticed.

Helene loves to criticize them after they've been to visit. She's always noticing something about them, or else interpreting something in a particular way, taking this as a sign that things aren't quite as they should be between them. I have to confess that her observations have been extremely keen, yes, almost eerily so at times, the awful implications she's managed to draw from one thing or another. For a while she was sure that it was only a matter of time before Elise would leave Hans-Jacob . . . or Hans-Jacob leave Elise . . . every time we all met . . . and it was as though her sympathies switched every other time, as though she alternated between seeing Elise's peevishness and inexhaustible self-pity with Hans-Jacob's eyes, and subsequently all of Hans-Jacob's bad sides with Elise's eyes in turn, his tiresome patronizing, his puerile whims, his indolence, his vindictive streak, his bad-tempered reprimands of Elise that would often ruin an entire game of bridge, if he was in a bad mood to start off with. And every single evening the four of us spent together, Helene found something new to get caught up in, a new piece to fit into the big picture that was constantly telling her that the two of them really didn't suit each other, that both of them were, in all likelihood, still just waiting for the right moment to leave the other one. When Kristoffer died it was almost as if she saw it as confirmation, nearly turning to me in triumph, the night Hans-Jacob rang, because now the opportunity had finally arisen to make the point, with the simple words she used to report the terrible news, that what was it she had said, she *knew* something would happen to that boy someday, the way they'd treated him since he was a baby!

But I'm not completely blameless either. Over the years I've been greatly entertained by Helene's interpretations and explanations, and I've also, to a certain degree, made my own contributions . . . maybe not so much to her actual criticism, but by way of certain insignificant remarks . . . the necessary affirmations she's needed in order to fully justify her reasoning. Indeed, of course . . . you're right, it did seem like that . . . that's probably true . . . a kind of confirmation of what she saw and the way she perceived it. I've certainly never had anything against Helene's interpretations, in the wake of Hans-Jacob and Elise's visits, of how things actually were between them, how they felt about themselves and one another. Even though these descriptions, or accounts, have with few exceptions been extremely negative, and thus haven't given Elise and Hans-Jacob much of a chance. When I think about it, I suppose I've pitched in with a few small observations of my own, in much the same vein as Helene's, over the years. It'd probably be accurate to say that at some point it became a pastime for the both of us, with Helene in the driver's seat mind you, this evaluation of Elise's and Hans-Jacob's marriage, examining and analysing it thoroughly based upon any new information that came to light. It simply became a habit that's lingered, even though it's lessened considerably, and which now as a rule limits itself to short statements, without further elaboration. Without the great pleasure either, in fact, that it once gave us.

Saturday evening, a few minutes after eight, just as I opened the door and saw Elise and Hans-Jacob standing there . . . motionless, in their coats and scarves, like a photograph from a faded album . . . I suddenly had to cough . . . a tingling itch in my throat was driving me crazy . . . and brought up an unexpected amount of phlegm that lay like an oyster at the very back of my tongue. Any words of welcome were out of the question, I just waved them in without saying a thing, careful to put on a friendly face so they wouldn't take my muteness to mean we weren't glad they'd come. I waited in the hall while they removed their coats and helped Elise hang hers up, the lump of phlegm still on my tongue: the thought that I may not be able to swallow it had made it impossible for me to make the attempt. Hans-Jacob soon started going on about the wine they'd brought, after first having handed me the bag, which was heavy and made a hollow clinking sound: it was a new type that had just come out, and in the end the only thing he probably didn't tell me about this formidable Rhine wine or whatever it was . . . and I'd say he really had to restrain himself in order not to . . . was that naturally it was also very expensive. It wasn't until they were on their way into the living room . . . I practically pushed them through the door . . . that I swallowed what in the meantime had grown to fill almost my entire mouth.

To prove that I hadn't lost the power of speech, I made a few casual remarks. But it didn't seem like either of them was really listening to what I said or even that they remembered that I hadn't said anything when they arrived. Hans-Jacob followed me when I went into the kitchen with the wine, stood with his legs apart in the doorway so I couldn't avoid listening to him while he took the ignoramuses to task, all the ignoramuses in the world, who buy wine for sixty or seventy kroners when all they had to do was spend ten or twenty kroners more in order to get something that was twice as good. That's how he likes to measure things, Hans-Jacob, half or twice as much, a third or seventy percent, seemingly irrefutable figures, whether the topic is politics, religion, or women.

We raised a toast, as usual, standing in the middle of the living-room floor like some secret brotherhood, gathered in the greatest confidentiality, and even exchanged a few small nods, some discreet glances, like well-drilled signals. The smell from Hans-Jacob, who was standing right beside me, was on the verge of making me vomit: he has a particular kind of eczema of the scalp that always itches and which Elise has attempted to cure with vinegar, so far without success, so that a mild odour always surrounds him, like his own peculiar little aura. Elise asked if the blouse she was wearing, an old one she'd inherited from her mother, was frightful and I said yes, that it was frightful, truly frightful, and I laughed as loud as the situation permitted. Hans-Jacob started going on about something that was in the news, I didn't catch what, but I soon thought there was something familiar about the opinions he was putting forward, as if I'd heard them before, just a little while ago. "Do you know what I mean?" he asked suddenly, and I was quick to nod: more than anything I wanted to put down my glass, put my arms around him, and squeeze it all out of him so that we could get it over with, and then we could make a start on something new, something fresh and unexpected, unfamiliar to us all. Perhaps he'd surrender completely in my arms if I did it, I thought, caught off guard by my sudden decisiveness? Perhaps if I squeezed hard enough, the air would go out of him as if he were a balloon, perhaps he'd empty completely, with a farting sound, so in the end I'd stand there with a slack little patch of skin between my hands, the sad remains of what was once Hans-Jacob Sandersen. It was impossible not to think of the words "hot air," I had thought them with regard to Hans-Jacob many times before, and now it was as though they had a new and greater meaning, as if they encompassed his entire person, the outer as well as the inner.

Then we ate, fondue with rice, chips, and vegetables. Elise and Hans-Jacob told us about a couple they knew via some friends, who they'd been to visit at a cottage down on the south coast somewhere, the man was an architect and had designed the cottage himself, or rather what seemed more like a fairy-tale castle than a cottage, if Elise's description was anything to go by. Why did they want to tell us about this? What interest could we have in a filthy rich, self-indulgent . . . at least judging by Hans-Jacob and Elise's portrayal of him . . . architect, of Swiss origin, who had obviously dazzled them all weekend long with his architectural escapades and exotic habits? It didn't take long before we got to hear about all the fantastic food they'd been served as well . . . *how rude, talking about another meal as they sat there eating food we'd served them* . . . but I decided not to let it show although to intimate nonetheless that their adventure down on the south coast didn't impress me much. Besides, I didn't like the impression they were giving, that for their part they didn't necessarily consider our friendship as being foremost, the one that would naturally take precedence in relation to their other friends and acquaintances. It was . . . I couldn't manage to interpret it any other way . . . as though they wanted to leave us in no doubt that they ate good food and had good times at other places too and not just at our house, that it was important for them to get this across.

"He's from Ticino," said Elise, and it was obvious that the name, which she could be fairly sure meant nothing to us, gave her a particular satisfaction, to be able to throw it out there as something self-evident, so self-evident and yet requiring, in our company, elaboration, as she well knew. Nevertheless I was prepared to deprive her of this pleasure by not asking. But to no avail. Trembling with the compulsion to inform, Elise asked the question herself: did this name not mean anything to us . . . ? And with that she had the excuse she needed in order to tell us that Ticino was a canton in the Italian-speaking part of Switzerland, and then this was followed by a whole load of details that I did my best to forget as soon as I heard them. I couldn't help imagining that it was the architect himself sitting there, with Elise's face as a mask, that he had snuck in, like a little demon, because it wasn't enough to hoodwink the friends of his friends, he had to slink along and prey upon their friends in turn, and then their friends, and so on. The demon's goal was world domination, and every living soul would know of his fairy-tale castle off Kragerø, his French wife who had her family send herbs and spices to her from back home, and his plans for a new type of architecture, in harmony with nature, inspired by modern theories about ecological agriculture. There was a bowl right in front of me on the table filled with green olives with red tongues sticking out at me. It was as though they were sitting there shouting at me every time I glanced at them: KRAGERØ! KRAGERØ! ARCHITECTURE! ARCHITECTURE! Switzerland had been my favourite country when I was small, I thought sternly. *But who the fuck had heard of Alfonso from Ticino?*

Contrary to our well-drilled procedure . . . it was around now I should have been using the last of my after-dinner energy to repair to my armchair without so much as a thought of getting up for the next couple of hours . . . I helped clear the table. I noticed, to my surprise . . . and perhaps that was why I broke with routine? . . . that I was nothing close to as full as I usually am, on the contrary my body felt oddly light on the march to and from the kitchen, a feeling I was not familiar with at all. Hans-Jacob on the other hand, had regained his customary weight, I saw him heave backward and forward a couple of times in his chair in order to pack himself firmly down between its arms properly. I was reluctant to do the same . . . thought with horror about the hours that now lay ahead of us. . . and saw to my dismay, by way of a stolen glance up at the kitchen clock the last time I turned around, that we'd eaten dinner even faster than usual: it was as though cruel fate had added an extra hour onto an ordeal I already knew would be unbearable.

But there was no way out. I pulled myself together and with a cheerful "all righty!" almost leaped into the chair in front of Hans-Jacob. It gave him a start, he'd probably expected me to exhibit the same listless contentment as himself. We each set about removing bits of food from our mouths with toothpicks and once again I marvelled at Hans-Jacob's strange habit of holding his free hand up in front of his mouth while he picked away with the other. His discretion has always irritated me, the hand shielding the view only draws your attention to what's going on behind it and makes it seem all the more vulgar. I thought about asking him how he'd gotten into this habit, but there was something about the atmosphere, I felt, that wouldn't quite allow it.

We sat in silence for a while. It looked like Hans-Jacob was pondering something, but for the moment he showed no sign of wanting to share it. We remained sitting like that for a good while, until my toothpick was broken into a multi-jointed worm, when suddenly we both opened our mouths to say something at the same time, which led to half-stifled gulps from the two of us and a new silence neither of us ventured to break. With a peremptory motion I let him know he could begin, an invitation he wasn't slow in taking up . . . *Hans-Jacob Sanderson be praised!* . . . because it was just dawning on me that I had no recollection whatsoever of what it was I'd been about to say.

"Yes," said Hans-Jacob. "I like a place inhabited by chatty women who voice opinions raucously, Andreas."

I didn't answer him right away, because I wasn't quite sure if I'd understood what he'd said . . . never mind what he actually meant . . . and it didn't help matters that he was now sitting there with a mysterious twinkle in his eye, as though he was observing my reaction, as if he thought he'd said something really clever. His lips twitched with an expectant smile, and I attempted to smile too, in the hope of coaxing him into saying something more, thinking the explanation might then be forthcoming. Instead he became deadly serious and the look he gave me seemed demanding, challenging almost, as if he required an immediate response to whatever it was he had come out with, and he wasn't willing, if I interpreted him correctly, to lift so much as a finger to help me out. I discovered I was sitting there motioning with one shoulder, without being aware of it, like a secret sign between partners in a card game, a message indicating that more information was necessary if I was to open correctly.

Finally, and this time so slowly that it seemed almost condescending, he said: "Yes, I like a place inhabited by chatty women who voice opinions raucously, Andreas."

I looked over toward the dining room table where their conversation was certainly lively, but they were far from being so boisterous that they could in any way be described as behaving "raucously." I waited as long as possible, but eventually turned to face Hans-Jacob again. At first he just stared at me, with a weary look as if he didn't really rate my chances of figuring out the little mystery he'd dropped in my lap. And then he repeated it, word for word, this time with such a long pause between each that it seemed there was a particular, and extremely important, meaning in every single word, a meaning which obviously should have sunken in by now.

"Yes. I. Like. A. Place. Inhabited. By. Chatty. Women. Who. Voice. Opinions. Raucously."

The final pause was the longest and most dramatic.

"Andreas."

Thoughts tumbled around in my head . . . I really didn't know what to do . . . if I should put my foot down and demand an explanation of his wordplay . . . or whether I had actually been momentarily distracted and let a valid point pass me by, one which under normal circumstances I would have understood instantly . . . after all we were pretty much on the same wavelength, Hans-Jacob and I, when it came to these kind of artful diversions, something we had been particularly fond of in our younger days. In any case my embarrassment had a paralysing effect. The only thing I could think of was to get up from the chair, on the pretext of having forgotten something, and walk out to the kitchen. I remained frozen in there, incapable of doing anything at all. The voices from the dining room sounded like a foreign language. It was as though I had stepped out of time and into a void, outside of everything else, where for the first time I was able, seriously able, to evaluate myself and my situation. And I thought: *I am never ever going to experience happiness again.* No, it was no thought, it was a certainty . . . an overwhelming and all-pervasive certainty that rose up inside me like a silent flood . . . *I am never ever going to experience happiness again.* I stood there a while, as if congealing in the matter of the thought. But finally I pulled myself together sufficiently to tear off a length of paper towel from above the cooker that I pressed against my face with both hands, drops of sweat gluing it to my forehead so it hung there on its own. "*Woooooooh,*" I said in a low voice, not so much because I thought I probably resembled a ghost with that white mask on my face as to see whether the vibration of my voice alone was enough to lift the paper up away from my mouth. It was, the paper flipped up without coming loose and falling, the edge flapping as though propelled by a little engine, tickling my lip. Then I became aware of the voices again, crumpled up my mask, and threw it as hard as I could at the pile of dirty dishes on the far corner of the countertop.

I had to bring something back with me, so I opened the fridge and looked carefully through all the shelves while my hopes gradually dwindled of finding anything that could justify my sudden departure from what was difficult to think of as a conversation, even though that's what Hans-Jacob for his part had meant it to be.

This'll have to do, I thought, and grabbed a half full carton of apple juice from the bottom shelf, swung the door closed with my foot, and walked as calmly as I could into the living room and sat down again, putting the carton down beside the cognac bottle without batting an eyelid. Hans-Jacob, completely motionless in his deep seat, looked as though he was still waiting for an answer.

"Cheers," I said.

We both raised our glasses, but we'd hardly set them down again before he resumed his unreasonable anticipation: now he seemed in better spirits, however, his eyes larger, his lips twitching a little, and then he peeped: "*Pi!*"

It sounded like a note from a child's flute.

I waited a moment, in case he said something more.

Then I said: "Yes?" And when he didn't answer: "Yes, yes, yes?"

Hans-Jacob gave another peep.

"Yes," I said, straining to make it sound like I was in the mood for joking around . . . as opposed to seizing him by the lapels and shaking him like a rag doll. "Yes, yes, yes."

"Pi!" said Hans-Jacob, and his tone was chipper; his face, on the other hand . . . almost expressionless.

"Yes," I said, determined to let him take the initiative. "Yes, yes, yes."

"Pi!" answered Hans-Jacob, even shriller than before, as if he was trying to imitate a bird.

"Yes," I said. "Yes, yes, yes."

"Pi!" he chirped and started to flap his wings.

"Yes," I said and tried stay calm. "Yes, yes, yes."

"Pi!" He shook when he said it, the pointy elbows of his jacket smacked hard against the leather of the armrests.

"Yes!" I shouted, leaped out of my chair, and before I knew it I'd saluted and was standing at attention. "Yes, yes, yes!"

"Pi!" chirped Hans-Jacob again and would probably have gotten up too, if he'd been able, but had to content himself with his cramped flapping.

"Yes!" I screamed, more fiercely than I'd intended, I saw Hans-Jacob give a start, and the voices behind us stopped . . . it was completely quiet in the living room for a little while . . . then the conversation over in the dining room continued, and I sat down again quickly in order to make my sudden outburst seem less shocking. But it seemed to have done the trick: Hans-Jacob finally removed his mask of mystery and seemed to be ready to consent to give me the long-awaited explanation.

"Pi," he said, holding three fingers in the air. "Three point one four. To thirteen decimal places."

He leaned back and slapped the armrests to applaud himself: "Thirteen decimal places," he repeated, squeezing his eyes shut while he nodded slowly a few times.

"Yes," I said, it was like my little refrain had a rhythm from which I couldn't quite manage to tear myself away: "Yes, yes, yes."

"Do you get it?" Hans-Jacob was in his element now, almost beaming: a wreath of brilliance around his unkempt mop of hair. "Each word represents a digit. The number of letters in the word indicates the digit. Do you see what I mean?"

I still didn't understand a thing.

"Yes. Three letters. Is equal to three."

He held up his fingers again. Then he bent his index finger into a hook and chopped at the air with it.

"Point!"

His fist, held in front of my face in an almost threatening manner.

"I."

His index finger.

"One. Like. Four. Yes, I like. Three point one four. See what I mean?"

It gradually began to dawn on me, but I almost didn't want it to become clear, just out of pure obstinacy . . . it was almost as though I preferred persisting in my ignorance at least a little longer, if for no other reason than to put a spoke in the wheel of Hans-Jacob's carefully planned coronation: I tried to remain as expressionless as I could.

"You see, this is something they've been doing for years, they're still doing it even now, calculating and calculating Pi, in order to extend its decimal representation, I wouldn't even dare to guess how far they've gotten nowadays. There've been whole books written on the subject. And as time has gone on it's become a game, making mnemonics out of as many numbers as possible. There are countless variations, in countless languages, each sentence more elegant than the next. The English and Americans are particularly adept at it."

Hans-Jacob took his pipe from his jacket pocket, bent forward with a little moan, turned the pipe over the ashtray and dug about in it with a little wooden scoop. The ash tumbled out along with a clump of fresh tobacco that now lay there on top of everything else, making it resemble a compost heap that had begun to bear fruit.

"But you see, Andreas, that's where we come into the picture."

"We," I thought, but didn't say anything. Hans-Jacob took out his tobacco pouch and packed the pipe, pressing down with a middle finger, which fitted perfectly into the little hole. Then he lit it: using the matchbox as a cover, a couple of puffs is sufficient, then he has it, a technique of his I've always admired . . . or envied him at least . . . since there's something about a man smoking a pipe, I've thought since I was a child, that gives the impression that he's master of everything under the sun, but which now, and it was with regret that I registered it, only sickened me with its affectation . . . the message it telegraphed . . . about being master of the world . . . a man about town . . . a *bon viveur* . . .

"Nobody's managed to come up with any such phrases in Norwegian, at least not any long enough to be of use. So I thought, well fuck that, that's not right. All things Norwegian happen to be in the ascendant at the moment and yet we lag behind in something so elementary. *Mathematica veritas*. What's wrong with people? Have they no imagination? So I sat down before we were about to go out tonight and put on my thinking cap, I'm telling you, Andreas, it didn't take me more than a couple of hours and then I had it! *Amat victoria curam*. To thirteen decimal places. I heard one in English once, I'm not quite man enough to remember it, but I think it was either to thirteen or fourteen decimal places and apparently that was considered one of the best. What do you think? A couple of hours on a Saturday afternoon, that's all it took."

He drew some slender curlicues in the air with his pipe, the smoke cloud clung to their shapes for a few seconds before vanishing.

"I was thinking of you, Andreas, since we were coming here, and I knew the ladies would start chatting away as soon as dinner was over. That everything would be just as it usually is. And then hey presto, I had it."

He gave a leisurely groan, as if the pipe was close to choking him with pleasure, before he repeated, voice quivering: "Yes, I like a place inhabited by chatty women who voice opinions raucously, Andreas."

I attempted to tally up the series of numbers in my head, but gave up.

"But if the comma is a decimal separator then there's one too many," I said. "At the end, before my name."

Hans-Jacob brushed my objection aside. "Jesus Christ, if you can manage to remember the sentence then I should think you'd able to overlook that! That's the whole point, Andreas, to be able to remember the number, to as many decimal places as possible. All you need to do now, if you want to impress some of your colleagues, is to make sure you etch this sentence into your brain, and then you can sit down anywhere and at any time and coolly and calmly write it down, number for number, Pi to thirteen decimal places. And of course you don't mention how you were able to remember it," he added, waving an admonitory finger, "I mean, *mano a mano*. See what I mean?"

If he says, "See what I mean?" one more time then I won't be held responsible for my actions, I thought. All the same, I had to admit, to my mild surprise, that I was becoming more and more occupied with the topic at hand, even if from a rather different angle than Hans-Jacob.

"But it's not even a particularly good sentence," I said, finally managing to put into words what, when all was said and done, probably bothered me the most.

"What do you mean?" asked Hans-Jacob.

"I mean, it's not something anyone would say, and just leave it at that."

"What?"

"That sentence of yours," I said. For a moment I considered trying to repeat it, but I knew that I'd make a mistake and that it wouldn't be taken graciously if I did. "Your mnemonic, the one about the women."

"But that doesn't matter, as long as you manage to remember it."

"No, but that's the problem, remembering it I mean. Because it's so . . . how should I put it?"

"So . . . ?" Hans-Jacob prompted, straightening up, making it look as though he was ready to go for my throat.

"It's just not something you would say, ordinarily. It's actually a pretty complicated line and that makes it almost impossible to remember. If it had been a more common phrase then it'd be easier, then you'd only need to remember the point of the phrase and then the words would come by themselves. But who's going to go around remembering . . . yes, you see, I can't remember it myself, even though you've said it so many times."

Hans-Jacob had a dark look in his eyes as he repeated the sentence, his pipe in his mouth, quite mechanically, without the optimistic tone he'd had at the beginning and which had probably been a genuine attempt on his part to hammer the words into me: "Yes, I like a place inhabited by chatty women who voice opinions raucously, Andreas."

"Well," I said, because even though I did want to play along, there was no way around the fact that Hans-Jacob's formula simply resisted being *etched into the brain*, as he'd put it. "I think that I, in any case, would need to write it down and always carry the piece of paper around with me if I was to have any chance of impressing someone with it."

Hans-Jacob's face turned red when he heard this, thick white tufts rose up from the pipe as if hurled from a catapult.

"And, you know, if you have to write it down anyway," I said, and I was now at liberty to amuse myself over my own obstinacy, "then it would be easier and take up less space to just write down the numbers themselves."

It wasn't easy to tell what was going on in my friend's head just then, in any case he was dumbfounded with . . . I don't know . . . disappointment . . . or shock that I hadn't simply gone along with the game . . . and maybe too he felt he hadn't gotten the recognition he thought he deserved in the wake of his ingenious contribution to arithmetic. He'd expected elation and enthusiasm and had been met with grumpy scepticism. But once I'd come out with guns blazing, there was no way I was prepared to ease off: Hans-Jacob, if anyone, should be man enough to stand it.

But now he just sat there, without saying a word: my last comments still hung in the air unanswered. For a moment I felt the taste of victory. Then I felt embarrassed by his silence. I looked at him. He sat there, slumped over, like a man defeated. I couldn't believe my eyes. I waited for him to lift his head and deliver a scathing retort. But no, he just sat there as if the power had been cut. All I wanted was a familiar quotation. A caustic reply. Something to rebuff my unwarranted scepticism and put me in my place. But he didn't say a word. He sat there as if paralysed. I felt like kicking him in order to wake him up. But I just sat there too, bewildered by the whole affair.

Suddenly he got up, not without some difficulty, and walked out into the hall. I heard him opening and closing the bathroom door. He left his pipe behind him, like a stranded submarine in the ashtray, the smoke visible as no more than an almost imperceptible trembling on the sofa behind it. I went out into the hall and looked for him . . . whatever use that was. The yellow light from the vestibule seemed as though it was radiating some kind of warmth, even though I knew this was only in my imagination. And I had a sudden vision of the toilet, spattered with blood, Hans-Jacob in convulsions on the floor with his wrists slit, his life pumping steadily out of him, his head turned up toward me with a look of confusion on his face while he whispered his last words. "I'm sorry, my friend. I'm sorry."

I sat there lost in thought when I suddenly realised that he was back again, sitting in the chair as if he'd never been out of it. There was nothing about him to suggest that he'd been out of sorts, on the contrary he appeared refreshed and in better form than he had been the entire evening: his little trip out to the toilet had obviously been a complete success, shaking off his melancholy and regaining his good old self. With a single deep drag he got his pipe going again, before he launched into an account about a colleague of his, hark hark, a foreigner, who was hired less than a year ago and of whom a good deal was expected, but there was also a bit of uncertainty, hark hark, about whether he was suited for the job, but pretty soon he'd proved himself a real *find*, as Hans-Jacob put it, and so I took it that he himself had played a part in picking him out, so everything he could think of saying in praise of this foreigner was in fact a reflection on him, an acknowledgment of his nose for talent. Apparently there were no limits to how gifted he was, this foreigner, and not only in the strictly professional sense, but, if I understood Hans-Jacob correctly, the man was almost *ingenious* by virtue of his *resourcefulness* and his *creative energy*, something the position clearly allowed him to make the most of.

I felt the need, however, to pick up our conversation where we had left off . . . even though I had no illusions about what this would result in . . . and how silly it would seem . . . still I put up my hand, as if trying to attract the teacher's attention. But Hans-Jacob was too engrossed in his own train of thought to take any notice of me . . . it would have taken a real shock to wake him, *rhetorically entranced* as he was. I sank back into my chair, I didn't know what else I could do. Hans-Jacob sat scratching his head while he spoke . . . it sounded like a dog chewing . . . and as he gradually got deeper into his story I felt my need to say something become more urgent . . . to ask about something at the very least . . . so it wouldn't seem like I'd fallen into a stupor. I considered several courses of action but rejected them, and while I sat there and watched Hans-Jacob's dizzying gesticulatory display . . . one thought alone cheered me up: *what if I jumped on top of him and bit his nose?* . . . and soon I was overcome by an irresistible urge to do just this, so much so that I had to hold myself back . . . I clung onto the armrests . . . I started salivating . . . *I imagined I could already feel that soft rubber thing between my teeth* . . . all I needed to do was to bite down, right until my jaws met . . . in desperation I looked around for some object or another to distract myself . . . then my thoughts turned to that young girl who'd been reported missing, perhaps I should interrupt and ask if he'd heard about the case and had formed any opinion on what could have happened. It made such an impression on me when I first heard the news . . . more than any of those other almost daily reminders of the evil in the world usually did . . . the trustworthy and laborious description, calmly delivered and completely devoid of drama, of how any fairly ordinary girl of that age would look . . . But I refrained, for fear of the case reminding him of what had happened to Kristoffer.

Then I realized that he still hadn't said which country he came from, the foreigner, on the subject of whom Hans-Jacob didn't seem to be anywhere near finished, and so I asked, almost in jest: "He's not Swiss, is he?"

"Yes, he's Swiss," answered Hans-Jacob, and it didn't seem like it struck him as a coincidence at all.

"From Ticino, by any chance?"

"Yes, He's from Ticino," answered Hans-Jacob as if this went without saying. "He came here with his wife last December. It looks like they're planning to settle down."

"So she's from around Ticino as well?"

"Indeed. They grew up together, so he says, and met when they were in high school."

"High school in Ticino?" I asked, thinking that this time the joke had to be obvious.

But Hans-Jacob was just as serious when he answered: "That's right, Ticino. A pretty small village, I think it was, right down on the border with Italy. I think he might have said that it was a Catholic high school, actually."

Almost unwittingly I'd started a conversation that Hans-Jacob seemed to find completely absorbing, and so I couldn't bring myself to stop. "Switzerland was my favourite country when I was a boy," I said, slightly uncertain as to whether I actually wanted to reveal this secret, as if I still . . . almost instinctively . . . wanted to avoid any topic that could possibly give Hans-Jacob an excuse to embarrass me. So I quickly added: "There've probably been quite a lot of people from Switzerland who've come here over the years and settled down. You wouldn't know it to look at them, anyway!"

"I suppose, though not so many that we don't still have plenty of room for them, in my view. Besides, you have to remember that they make good use of themselves, the Swiss, no matter where in the world they wind up. Work like Trojans! Real naturals when it comes to turning a profit!"

"God, I didn't mean it like that."

"We should only be grateful, shouldn't we, so long as it's from that part of the world they're coming from, all those people desperate to get their foot in the door. It's the other ones we need to watch out for."

"Without a doubt. But that wasn't what I had in mind when I said it."

"Yes, Andreas, I'd go as far as to say that the more Swiss people live in a country then the greater the chances of things going well for that country. Perhaps the number of Swiss is an approximate gauge of the economic health of a nation, who knows? That for every Swiss person in full-time employment the gross domestic product increases by such and such. It'd be amusing to attempt some calculations on that subject. I tell you it's the first thing I would have done if I was made head of state of one of those hopeless countries in the Balkans, imported a handful of Swiss people straight away, then you wouldn't have to wait long to see the result, things would begin to thrive overnight."

Hans-Jacob got up from the chair and proclaimed: "A Swiss a day keeps the trouble away!"

He didn't remain standing any longer than gravity allowed him and fell back down with a thud followed by a hollow cracking sound as the chair tipped over, Hans-Jacob had to cling onto the armrests so as not to be thrown out of it: one leg was broken and the foot jutted out from under the seat like a bone.

We got up to inspect the damage. It turned out that the leg of the chair could easily be slotted back into place where it had cracked off and still bear the weight, of the chair anyway, if not of Hans-Jacob, until it was repaired. Hans-Jacob sat down gingerly, gradually lowering his full weight into place, until he was sitting as before, albeit not quite so relaxed.

"The ski slopes in that part of the country are magnificent," he said, as if nothing had happened, not even a broken chair could knock him off his stride. "Even better than all the more famous places, so those in the know tell me anyway, since there're so many people around now, on the piste and everywhere else, that you don't get to make full use of the facilities anyway."

No sooner had he said this than the leg of the chair gave way again, only this time it broke right off and rolled out onto the floor, though its collapse wasn't enough to unseat Hans-Jacob: seemingly unperturbed by the mishap, he merely leaned slightly over to one side in order to compensate for the imbalance. "But that's the price you pay in order to earn a reputation," he went on. "It's sad, but that's the way it is."

"So it's probably only a question of time then," I said, "before the best spots in Ticino become as well known and are overrun by every Tom, Dick, and Harry as well."

"*Certainement*," replied Hans-Jacob. "*Certainement*. If you want to keep the best places to yourself then you better get a move on, I tell you."

He fixed his eyes on me so suddenly it nearly made me jump: "But what about you, Andreas," he said, "what's at the top of *your* wish list?"

After the door slammed shut it was like this new silence erased all trace of them. I had to restrain myself from giving a loud cheer. I pulled off my tie, which slid off from around my neck like a snake . . . undid the top button of my shirt . . . walked over to the big window . . . and submerged my gaze in the sea of glittering lights. I thought about the missing girl again, and it wasn't so much grief or fear on the family's behalf. . . who at that moment were sitting together in a room someplace or another in the city staring at the telephone . . . that I felt . . . but a kind of resignation, fatigue, and powerlessness at the thought of how exceedingly little it takes before everything you've built your existence upon is snatched away from you, or destroyed. I saw Hans-Jacob and Elise drift out of the darkness and across the courtyard, looking like they didn't have any legs. For some reason or another I was convinced that they were talking disparagingly about me.

I stared at the grey discs cast by the lights in front of the garages. If something were to happen down there, I thought . . . if someone tried to force one of the garage doors . . . or a person was attacked and robbed, if someone tried to rape a young girl . . . what an infinite distance there'd be between any possible compulsion I might feel to intervene and save someone and the actual practical possibility of me carrying out some kind of *deed*. I thought about the door that was locked after Elise and Hans-Jacob, the lift that in all probability was at the ground floor and would take forever to get up here to the seventh floor, all this would lie between the screaming woman and myself. I pictured Elise as this woman, Hans-Jacob lying in a pool of blood on the ground beside her, and I tried to imagine my most likely reaction without reaching any conclusion with which I felt I could be satisfied. No, I simply had no idea what I would do. And suddenly I wished the whole evening undone. That they had never come, that it had been an ordinary Saturday . . . spent in front of the television . . . and if I had to be completely honest, I'd prefer it was a quite a while before Elise and Hans-Jacob came to visit us again.

Reluctantly I went into the bathroom, into a white world of rattling sounds, scented creams, loud frothy toothpaste that smelled like freshly tapped beer. I felt an urge to unburden myself, to shake off everything that was weighing upon me before we went to bed, but there was something about the purity in there, *the sanitary atmosphere* that kept me from doing it and made me feel dirty. For a moment I considered abandoning my principles and having a bath. But as soon as I stood beside the bathtub and looked down at it the horrible thought of lying in a coffin came over me again. I remembered how once I'd had a bath after being bedridden for a long time, when I was finished there were flakes of skin floating on the water like a thick porridge, so many of them that they covered the whole surface and made it look like an entire person had dissolved . . . I let the water out and hosed down the remains and couldn't shake the feeling of wiping out the traces left by a crime . . . someone had been done away with in the most horrible way . . .

I must have stood lost in my own thoughts for a while, because a sarcastic voice demanded to know what I was hoping to catch sight of down there. I turned around and began to unbutton the rest of my shirt, slowly, as if deep down I was hoping to be interrupted. I began to tell a story from my schooldays . . . just a whim? . . . something that I said I'd completely forgotten, and which Hans-Jacob had mentioned in the course of the evening . . . and that much was true . . . but even I could hear, as I was telling it, that it wasn't a particularly good story, and so I hurried to finish it. All the same I think the main reason I told it was because I felt the need to put the evening in a better light, that I wanted to shift attention away from my strange behaviour and the fact that my conversation with Hans-Jacob had become quite strained after a while, almost coming to a complete stop on a couple of occasions, as if we suddenly didn't have anything to say to one another, and neither of us could serve up an appropriate reminiscence that could release us from our awkward silence, and I couldn't deceive myself that this slightly strained atmosphere had gone unnoticed, and this was probably why I felt the need to fix it, to demonstrate that no matter how it may have appeared, it had actually been a very pleasant evening. In any case my story didn't make much of an impression, her only response being: "She was talking about Kristoffer again tonight."

"Oh?" I said, grateful, to an extent, for the interruption. I thought with horror about having to be the one to sit there an entire evening listening to Elise in her peculiar grief. Still almost proud, it seems, even today, as she relates the details of the accident, expounds upon all the terrible facts . . . *terrible, because they were so haphazard* . . . with the particular authority of someone who's been subjected to real tragedy, about what it's like to be affected by something like that, how it feels when someone close is taken from you, brutally and without warning. The loss of Kristoffer has become for her the yardstick for all accidents, how serious they are, how much they could be said to have affected the bereaved, all in all, and thus whether or not it's beneath her dignity to feel compassion. And if Elise hears about other misfortunes that surpass her own . . . if Helene or I on a rare occasion have been able to tell her about someone we know, or have heard of, who's been through something so unimaginably horrible that to question it would be perceived as offensive . . . then she seems to really take it to heart . . . as if she believes we're saying it in order to mock her, that we're criticising her by implying that Kristoffer's accident wasn't so exceptional as she'd like to think, after all.

"She lives and breathes for that boy, even though he's dead."

I kicked a space for my feet and drew the duvet tight over my shoulders but still felt oddly uncomfortable when I'd finished re-arranging things, as if there wasn't quite room for me under the covers. I did a few pelvic exercises, as I usually do, they're supposed to be good for the prostate as long as you start doing them early enough. Then I thought about other, more pleasant things I could do. Sometimes I imagine myself in a dangerous situation, in a city under siege, starved and under constant fire . . . or in a wind-swept cabin in winter, like the one Chaplin was in, on the edge of the cliff . . . or that I'm on my deathbed, either in a hospital or here at home, with my family and friends around me weeping . . . in order to calm my nerves before I fall asleep, or just for the fun of it, if I think that it's going to take me a while to doze off. One time I had a fever and I gave an hour-long lecture on the best way to tackle the problem of unemployment. I couldn't remember any of it the next day, but I did remember that it was fantastic. There's something strangely relaxing and comforting about lying com-pletely still and at the same time creating so much drama and ex-citement around yourself, pushing yourself to the limit while you just lie there, deaf to this world, until your body stiffens and sort of withers away under your brain. Or I write the first chapter of a thriller that never gets any farther. They're fairly banal, most of my nocturnal adventures, and it'd be very embarrassing if somehow or other they found their way up into the real world, parading around as an example of the innermost workings of their originator's mind. But fortunately it's inconceivable that they would. It might be the siege of a mediaeval castle one night, or an action movie along the lines of James Bond. But it's as though the banality of these scenarios is precisely what makes them so refreshing, makes for such a liberating and stimulating experience . . . to immerse yourself, become completely engrossed, safe in the knowledge that their almost inexcusably naïve content is exempt from any moral responsibility, any intellectual or political norm.

I imagined I was the father of the young girl who had gone missing . . . that we were reunited after the police had managed to wrest her from the arms of a crazed sex killer . . . I just about managed to hold back the tears . . . Later I attempted a variant on the snowed-in gold-miner in no-man's-land, or else that I was a fugitive who had been forced to seek refuge in that same cabin, a criminal with a price on his head and a reward being offered just for information that could lead to his arrest. But soon I had to give up, the calm I required in order to get going properly, the concentration that was necessary in order to bring things to a successful conclusion was far beyond my reach. I was just as restless now as I had been before we went to bed, no, more so now, because the silence and the darkness around me and the cool wind from the gap in the curtains were utterly ruthless in forcing me to surrender myself, offering me no opportunity to discount them as fiction . . . I mean those insomniac night-thoughts, they alone hold the field. And suddenly I became aware of how fast my mind was racing . . .

from one thing to the other at a furious pace, without me being able to hold on to a single thought . . . they changed incessantly . . . like train after train at a shunting yard . . . I put my hand to my head . . . and I felt it throbbing . . . and I thought, now I'm thinking . . . this is what it's like to think . . . and then I thought that if I concentrated all my attention on thinking then perhaps I'd manage to hold on to this one thought and not deal with everything at once . . . but the thought of thinking soon just made me think of a whole bunch of other things that my one thought might grapple with . . .

I opened my eyes and stared up at the dusky blue ceiling . . . the lamp like a protruding eye in the centre . . . and suddenly it seemed infinitely distant, the square ceiling boards, the round lamp, the corners where the walls and ceiling meet . . . as if it were a hundred metres up . . . I shifted my gaze . . . to the grey wardrobe a hundred metres away, the wallpaper with the green pears on it a hundred metres away. I placed my hand on her hip . . . at one time I couldn't sleep unless I had my hand there . . . it was as if I clung on tight so as not to disappear completely. And I noticed it was slightly reassuring, the round shape, the gauzy material, the swaying movement. The distance to the roof however was just as great, it was as though I were sinking deeper and deeper down into the pillow. I considered switching on the light . . . I got it into my head that it was the only way to chase away these eerie occurrences . . . but thought that it would cause too much commotion over nothing.

I thought about Marit and about what I had said to her that day we met. It struck me how idiotic I had been: a groan of embarrassment escaped my lips as I brought it to mind again. Then I became anxious: what if she had let word get around about the surprise news her father had announced? Perhaps a considerable number of people had heard about it already. I couldn't ignore the fact that her and Karl-Martin's acquaintances included the children of friends of ours or people who were on good terms with our friends' children, so that the news would also find its way to them, eventually, like a poisonous snake slithering along . . . If she was to tell someone, confide in some close friends, then maybe it wasn't inconceivable that she'd present it as *happy news?* . . . then I wouldn't know what to feel. Happiness . . . or inconsolable dejection? In any case it wasn't too encouraging to think that what I'd told her was so *utterly implausible*, so far removed from reality. And yet that was probably exactly how Marit had perceived it too, as something *utterly implausible*. Yes, maybe that was exactly how it was, maybe I didn't need to worry about whether the lie would one day boomerang back on us after first having smashed to pieces what little respectability we had left . . . simply because Marit hadn't for a moment believed a word I'd said, no, on the contrary . . . and she'd be terribly sceptical in any case, due to the knowledge she had . . . and which must still be lingering despite the intervening years . . . of her mother and father and the life they led . . . so that she . . . irrespective of what she herself might think . . . would under no circumstances allow the news to reach anyone else's ears. Not even Karl-Martin's, with whom I took it for granted she had a rather chilly and distant relationship.

I became increasingly dejected at the thought of how implausible it must have seemed. I tried to think of a possible reason for us to want to leave each other, Helene and I, but couldn't come up with any, not one that sprang immediately to mind anyway. Christ, I thought, was there really nothing about my life or Helene's life . . . or rather our life together . . . which could make such a breakup probable? Perhaps for Marit and Nina their parents' marriage represented some kind of last impregnable bastion? That whatever else may happen, surely nothing would happen to *that*? But then how could she have acted so indifferently when I told her? But I'd seen that she was upset . . . I'd seen it . . . it had seemed, for a fleeting moment, that she was at a loss for what to do. Still, it couldn't have been that bad or she wouldn't have been able to shake it off like she did. Maybe she'd forgotten it already, what did I know? Or was she walking around mulling it over right now, wondering, at this very moment, whether what I'd told her in confidence was true or not?

Nina, I thought. What would she say? And I tried to imagine what her reaction would be . . . what her most likely reaction would be . . . *would have been* . . . if it had been her I'd blurted it out to . . . completely different from Marit's, I was convinced of that. She probably would have seen right through me, I thought . . . maybe right away . . . and posed a simple question, objected in a simple way which would have been sufficient to blow a hole in my deception so that I'd be forced to go back on it immediately, before it was too late, admit that it was inane drivel, wave it away as quickly as it had come, with her help, and as a blessing for both of us, and then we could have sat a while longer, and not been forced to part like myself and Marit, since my idiotic impulse, unchallenged as it was, had made it as impossible for Marit as for me to continue to take our conversation seriously. Why hadn't she questioned me? I thought. And now I was absolutely certain that that's what Nina would have done in her place. Yes, without a doubt, she would have.

I thought . . . out of sheer spite perhaps . . . about how easy it would be to actually do it. That no matter how little it would be to my advantage, it would be the easiest thing in the world for me to walk out of here without a second look, never to return. Suddenly I was lying shivering with impatience in the warm hollow under the duvet. I wanted to leave her, right there and then, wake her up with a roar, tell her that it was over, end our marriage immediately, grab a few things and leave her, leave everything behind me never to see it again, casting one last triumphant look at these familiar places, the bedroom and the living room, the hall, the ghastly wallpaper that should have been changed ages ago, all the meaningless stuff that's piled up over the years, shelves and shelves of it, the innumerable side tables that are good for nothing but covering in bric-a-brac . . . and which I'd never again . . . never again . . . need to have an opinion on . . . My hand trembled on her hip, my nails quivered against the gauzy material that separated them from her fleshy flank. I felt an irresistible urge to scratch and scrape her until she bled. The muscle felt like an evil string running up my arm, quivering, dying to get to work. I tried to get control of it, compose myself, prevent myself from doing something I knew I'd have great difficulty apologizing for. Christ, what had come over me? I felt infuriated, crazed. How did this happen? I was lying motionless, in the foetal position, as if I was fast asleep, but on the inside I was boiling with rage. How was this possible?

Before I knew it I'd lifted my hand up under the duvet, made a fist, and hit Helene as hard as I could on the hip. She let out a scream, turned in the bed like an animal caught off guard and suddenly under threat. But by then I'd already withdrawn my hand. I lay with my face turned away and pretended to be asleep . . . and managed, despite all the excitement to force myself to breathe in a regular, heavy, and seemingly imperturbable rhythm.

"Andreas?"

It rang out like a shot in the silence, that sharp voice.

Her hand moved across and gently rocked my shoulder.

"Andreas?"

There was a pressure on my chest, as if my lungs were about to explode . . . but then it vanished, like a gentle rain drizzling down my body.

"Andreas?" she repeated, but lower now, as if she'd already resigned herself to the fact that I was asleep.

But still it took a long time before she let go of me, I felt her behind me like an immense figure, towering like a sphinx, watching . . . still? . . . for signs of life, something that would expose my sleep as false. I didn't move a muscle. Eventually I heard her gather the duvet around her and felt the bed rocking as she turned to settle back down. Then it was quiet. And in this silence my choked excitement slowly turned into nausea: my throat tightened, I felt a pressure in my jaws, a trembling between my eyes that made me dizzy, for a moment it was as though I wouldn't manage to hold it back. And only now did I become aware of how cold the room was, noticeably colder than last night, the curtains cutting into each other with a tremulous sound.

After a dark, dull, soundless Sunday that seemed like it would never end, I woke up on Monday morning and as usual I couldn't remember what I had dreamt, but I noticed that the dream had made an unforgettable impression on me all the same: every breath I took now felt as though it needed to be willed, to be thought through. But the icy-cold morning soon helped bring me around, I felt a bit calmer as soon as I got outside. Or was this calm simply some form of indifference? I stood for a while waiting for the green man at the traffic lights by the tram stop, impatient, I noticed, to get on with the business of the day. I stood there for what seemed like an eternity, while the cold made the hairs on the back of my neck stand on end.

"COME HERE!" somebody suddenly screamed right in my ear, giving me such a start that I nearly dropped my bag, and I looked around in alarm, prepared, I realized, to obey whomever it was standing there. But it was just an elderly gentleman with a dachshund on the other end of a taut leash, it pulled and he pulled, they were like two children fighting over a toy. He screamed again, the owner, and suddenly the animal decided to obey: the gentleman in the double-breasted overcoat narrowly avoided hitting the ground with a thud.

Things improved when I got to work and put my hairnet on, almost like it squeezed some of the queasiness out of me.

Contrary to my routine I neglected to turn on the light and took a stroll around in the darkness between the machines, running my fingers over them gently and inhaling the smell of dust, oil, and paper. My eyes adjusted to the gloom and I wished that we could do a whole days' work there in the dark, never switching the lights on. I had to laugh at the thought of Kåre and Jens-Olav and Arne fumbling about in the semi-darkness from machine to machine. And Didriksen, who wouldn't be able to see his hand in front of his face when he came down here from the rock-candy white of upstairs: between that and the noise of the machines there'd be no chance he could ever orient himself, it would be as though he'd fallen into a bottomless blackness, or stumbled off the edge of a cliff. I pictured myself and a couple of the guys standing on either side of the door waiting for him, jumping him as soon as he opened it and giving him a good beating before we walked out leaving him lying battered and bruised in the pitch-darkness, the machines still running, left on in order to reinforce Didriksen's feeling of doom. Before we left I would bend down and whisper in his ear: "That was for Schiong, you filthy rat."

Then I heard someone speak, and it made me jump, I was so confused that I didn't actually know where on the factory floor I'd ended up. I recognised the voices of Jens-Olav and Gunnar, coming from the changing room. I ran around and turned on all the machines, finally pushing the button on number five, the last one . . . for a moment it seemed as though it had swallowed my thumb because the button is protected by thick, yellow rubber . . . directly under Didriksen's peephole, just as the last flash of light snapped into place and the whole workshop was, finally, illuminated, everything in order in the wonderful hum from all nine machines. I made it, but only just. Jens-Olav and Gunnar stood in the doorway in their dustcoats and hairnets. And it looked as though Jens-Olav was surprised to see me just standing there, not busy with anything.

Around ten o'clock Didriksen came down to inspect things . . . or pretend to inspect things . . . with rolled-up shirtsleeves and those square glasses of his, which he probably wears because he thinks they make him look busy and important, though none of us ever saw him do anything to indicate that he needed them, at any rate. Eventually he made his way over to me, just stood there for a while looking at me . . . his arms, which were covered in tiny sores from the flies, hung uselessly on either side of him, as if they belonged to someone else. Finally he said, "And everything's running smoothly here?" and I couldn't escape the thought that there was something more to his question today than usual . . . as if it bore the imprint of being an actual question rather than the clear statement in the form of a question I usually perceived it as. Yes, it was as though he was standing there really waiting for an answer, like he wasn't sure anymore if it was the case that things were running smoothly, which he'd been able to confirm so many times in the past. How should I answer? How do you answer a question like that? Was it supposed to be a hint? A discreet appeal? Was there something he wanted me to understand, something he couldn't get himself to say in so many words, at least not out here? I thought of his wife, maybe something had happened to her since the last time we spoke . . . maybe this was what he wanted to get across. Kristine, I thought . . . Kristine Didriksen . . . and still I couldn't quite make myself believe that this woman existed . . . Had her condition deteriorated . . . or improved? Was that what he wanted to tell me? Was it good news trying to force its way out? A breakthrough that had given cause for optimism . . . or yet another setback? I didn't envy him, having to live from day to day with that kind of uncertainty. But neither could I bring myself to feel any real sympathy for him as he stood there, his glasses clamped so hard onto the tip of his nose that it looked as if there was a little protuberance right on the end, white as a peeled almond. For a moment I thought he was going to say something else, it looked like he was standing there summoning strength for the final push: I thought that I'd surely be able to manage the situation, come what may. It was as though I had a sudden surplus of energy . . . I felt capable of taking responsibility for whatever it might be, yes, it was as though deep down I *wanted* the man to break down on the floor, right in front of me, sobbing in despair, clinging onto my trouser leg, so I could prove to the world how I handled myself in a crisis. But then he hobbled off and disappeared up the stairs, back to his flies.

I kept working, quietly and effectively, but wondered about the hollow feeling I had in my chest . . . it went right up to my throat . . . as if my gullet was bigger than usual. It's my nerves, I told myself, without thinking it sounded particularly convincing. It felt as though I was irritated about something that in reality was a purely physical discomfort . . . or the opposite, that it was a frustration that was manifesting itself in an itchy, nauseated feeling . . . maybe I was disappointed Didriksen's breakdown never materialized? It almost felt like he'd let me down, at the critical moment

he had destroyed a golden opportunity . . . Then I stopped myself.
I thought about his wife, or at least tried to turn my thoughts to
her . . . I tried as hard as I could to feel compassion for her . . . for
both of them . . . for *him*, because when it came down to it he was
probably the worse off of the two . . . yet again with rather meagre
results as far as the larger emotions were concerned . . . And an
unpleasant thought struck me, a suspicion levelled at myself, that
if I'd received news of someone's death right now, then it wouldn't
have made any impression on me, no matter who it might have
been. I thought . . . yes, I was almost certain that if I'd received a
telegram right that minute, bearing devastating news . . . that my
sister was dead . . . or that Helene had been informed that she was
seriously ill and was now lying in a hospital in a sea of bandages
and cables . . . that Elise and Hans-Jacob had died in a car crash .
. . then it wouldn't have made any impression on me at all, *I would
have simply folded the telegram together, put it in my pocket, and
continued my work from where I'd left off.* Or if I learned that either Marit or Nina were missing, had vanished without trace, that
there was a suspicion of criminal involvement . . .

Gunnar came over to me during break and told me a terrible story
about someone he knew, or had known, or had known *of* in any
case. He put his hand on my shoulder when he got to the point,
despite the fact that he was talking so loudly that everyone else
couldn't help but hear. As usual, Gunnar's tendency to confide
made me feel pretty ill at ease. It's a nuisance that he's so open
about things. At any moment he's liable to blurt out secrets that

other people would have spent years working up the courage to admit. I've never liked talking to him, I always feel uncomfortable about the way he leans into me . . . in order to get as close as possible, presumably. Besides, his face is so thin that you can't really see what he looks like until you catch him in profile.

So I gave a sigh of relief when he crumpled up his sandwich paper and got up to go over to the coffee machine for a refill. The radio was on low in the background, nobody said anything, probably because they'd all been sitting listening to Gunnar. Whereas usually there was lively discussion about even the most trivial of subjects, now it was completely quiet, no not quiet, hushed. Everyone sat there chewing, their jaws grinding slowly, like millwheels. The atmosphere in the break room suddenly felt unbearable. For a moment I considered drawing my colleagues into a discussion of that news story about the missing girl, and then discreetly leaving them to it . . . there was lots to talk about if you really got into it . . . but instead I stood up, without saying anything, and walked out into the hall in the direction of the toilets. My chest ached. I tried to belch in order to relieve the pressure, and it helped a little, but then my chest sort of swelled up again . . . as if my body was holding my breath against my will. When I got into the bathroom I walked right over to the mirror and began making faces in it, as twisted and as ugly as I was able: stuck my front teeth out like a rabbit, puckered up my nose, opened my eyes wide and made myself cross-eyed until I felt the first jolts of nausea, and was just as alarmed as I was satisfied over how unrecognisable I looked, even to myself. Then I locked myself into the only stall in there, pulled down my trousers, and sat on the seat. I looked at my watch. I could only sit in here so long before they'd start to wonder what was up. I squeezed out a few drops of piss, not because I needed to, but to have something to do. I looked at my watch and tried again. I looked up along the wall, green with countless little nubs of concrete, and high up, beyond the immediate field of vision of someone sitting on the toilet, I thought I could make out the beginning of a word . . . yes . . . an obscene word . . . good grief . . . that someone had, rather unsuccessfully, attempted to scratch onto the rugged surface, which was obviously not well suited for such confidences. I realized that it actually had to be the work of one of my colleagues, and then I noticed that this had somehow put my mind at ease, the thought that one of them . . . who on earth could it have been? . . . had gone and defied every notion of respectability . . . which we all have in common . . . *and in a moment of childish excess had taken out some sort of sharp object from his pocket and stood there scraping for dear life.* He must have had one foot on the toilet seat . . . his upper body braced against the stall's door . . . hovering almost . . . it was the only way he could have reached so high. I thought that if I could only manage to find out who it had been, then that person would undergo a transformation, right before my eyes, and it would be a lasting change, for all time, he'd never be himself again. And if everyone found out about it, then he would, in all probability, have to quit right there and then.

Without warning, someone tried the handle. I jumped up and fumbled with my trousers, even though I knew the door was locked. My hands were shaking as I tried to do up my fly and buckle my belt, and I pulled the chain so that whomever was out there wouldn't get the impression that I was just sitting there when I knew there was someone else who needed to use the facilities. Under cover of the flushing sound, I finished getting dressed and putting myself in order, so that, calm and collected and, I thought to myself, with a clear conscience, I could open the door and meet this person. Who was nowhere to be seen. Who must have gotten tired of waiting and left with his business unfinished. Had I really taken such a long time to get my pants on? And for a moment it felt as though I had lost all sense of time.

I took my time in the corridor, looked at a couple of the outdated calendars from the company suppliers, and expected to be met with a steady buzz of voices, when to my alarm I discovered that the lunchroom was empty, that there wasn't a single person there, that the radio was turned off, the table cleared . . . it seemed as if there hadn't been anyone there in days. I looked up at the clock above the door, twenty-five to, which I immediately confirmed by my own watch: "Good God!" I groaned aloud to myself, hurried down the corridor again, and pushed open the workshop door, making it slam into the wall with a bang. Jens-Olav was already there pouring oil into number three, even though he knew as well as I did that it could easily be left for another fifteen or thirty minutes. But maybe he didn't trust me anymore . . . after my odd little exit from the lunchroom? Was he the one who'd tried the door, in order to check if that was where I was hiding? Yes, of course, I thought: the lunch break was over, I hadn't shown up again, they'd talked among themselves about where I could have gotten to, one of them, Jens-Olav, had hurried out to the lavatory in order to look for me. And I thought: This is what you get for being faithful to the minute, as reliable and punctual as clockwork, your whole life . . . the one day you're the *tiniest little bit behind schedule*, what a catastrophe, there's no limit to how badly they'll misinterpret it . . . even the slightest misdemeanour or memory lapse and that golden thread of trust, which has been laboriously spun for so many years, snaps *right in two*. It takes nothing at all, for someone who's always done the right thing. I got the oilcan from Jens-Olav, perhaps a bit more abruptly than intended, and waved my hand to signal that I'd take care of it, just get back to your own work. He stared at me in confusion, looked around with his customary, aggrieved expression, shrugged his shoulders, and went back to number two. When I turned to face Heljesen, who was standing nearest to me, he looked away just as I looked up.

Around two I thought I heard a skidding sound. Instead of checking the pressure on my machine, which would have been the natural thing to do, I looked around, to see if any of the others had heard it too. Then I wasn't sure, the sound had disappeared . . . if there'd been a sound at all? . . . and then I noticed that the pressure, according to the gauge that I eventually, almost reluctantly, had to take a look at, was at a slightly higher level than usual. I circled around the machine for a while, carrying out various little adjustments in order to try and catch that sound again, but I couldn't hear anything unusual in its steady, deep drone. The needle in the pressure gauge, meanwhile, had risen further when I checked it again. Not by much, but enough that I finally decided to open up the side and take a look, just to be on the safe side. I went into the

storeroom to get some tools . . . past Hans-Jacob who was standing manning the grinder . . . and I don't know why, but I suddenly
felt like one of those young volunteers at those big sporting events
who, because they're delighted to be there, carry out their simple
duties with an eagerness that's the absolute antithesis of the ath-
letes' professional calm.

I took out a hammer and banged a little on the front cover of my
machine. Then I stood, hammer in hand, and just looked. I could
feel Heljesen's eyes on the back of my neck, and glanced around
in order to see if there was anyone else staring. There wasn't. I
brought the hammer down on top of the cover . . . making such an
awful clatter that I was almost afraid I'd broken something . . . and
spun around, and caught Heljesen in the act, before he had time to
look away. He'd been busy opening some boxes, and now he bent
over, as if that was what he was on his way to do anyway, and cut
off the plastic bands with a Stanley knife. I could see that he was
sweating, two parallel streaks ran from the cord of his hairnet diagonally across his cheek, stopping at the wing of his nose, making
a glistening crescent. I listened, but didn't hear anything out of the
ordinary . . . a deep, reverberating rumble . . . I hit the cover again,
not as hard this time. Then I pretended to bend down for something while I looked under my arm in the Heljesen's direction: he
stood there staring as if he'd seen a ghost. I straightened up, dizzy
from all the blood that had gone to my head. If he looks at me
like that one more time, I thought . . . but left the thought unfinished. Still, something should be done about him, I thought . . .
someone should give that nitpicker a piece of their mind . . . put
him in his place, once and for all . . . he's so particular about mak-

ing sure things are done *fair and square*, as he says himself . . . in the most painstaking and protracted way that I've ever seen . . . and which in reality only leads to him working *twice as slowly* as the rest of us, even though what we're doing isn't so different, and our end results are in no way inferior to his. If I was the boss I would've given him a talking to a long time ago, for needless time wasting. What's the point in spending an hour being thorough when you can get the job done in half an hour and still be sure it's good enough? As well as that he's got a habit of pushing his tongue down against his bottom teeth when he's concentrating, so that his jaw sticks out a good deal more than usual. Good God, I thought. A little bit of effort and it's like he slips several rungs down the evolutionary ladder.

I hammered away at the cover over the valve, where I knew it wouldn't cause much damage, but where it made an awful clatter, resounding like cymbals. Then I turned to face Heljesen, slowly, triumphantly almost, and when our eyes met . . . his fearful, mine ice-cold . . . I got it into my head that that was exactly what I had done, *called him an ape*, when I'd walked by him with the tool earlier. I knew that'd been what I was thinking, and not for the first time, the truth was I thought about it every time I saw Heljesen bent over something, it was impossible not to think of it, no one who saw him like that, his whole jaw protruding like some primitive beast's, could help but think it, I was sure of that. Everyone here, Didriksen included, must in all likelihood have thought *you ape* every time they saw him working on something, maybe they did it every time they saw him no matter what, because they'd started to associate him with that hideous grimace, whether or not it was on his face at the time. It's a wonder no one has said it to him yet, I thought, and for a moment I was tempted to remedy the situation. *Or hit him over the head with something hard.* As good as anything, I thought, feeling the weight of temptation in my hand. Plant the hammer in his head. It'd suit him, seeing how he's always bragging about how practical he is.

I pictured it again, the half word up on the toilet wall. Was I really the only one . . . *apart from whoever had written it* . . . who'd noticed it? I hadn't ever done so myself, before today. Discovered or not, it was as though that amputated obscenity had managed to drive a wedge between us, upsetting that natural harmony within the company. We'd always been on good terms with each other, I thought, my workmates and me . . . so the thought never occurred to me, not even as a remote possibility, that something might come between us, something that could make it difficult for us to work in the same room. Our unwavering routines were such a part of me that I had never wanted anyone to quit, anybody new to start, there to be any changes, rearrangements, cutbacks, expansions, to disturb the perfect balance that had always existed between us, how we'd divided up tasks between ourselves and how, all in all, everything functioned like a little hill of hardworking ants, quite similar, quite carefree, even . . . as secure I think as you can hope to feel. That was how it was. That was how it had to be.

I wondered about my chances of getting a new job, if I was to quit this one. The problem was there weren't many places that still did things the old way. And if it was necessary to retrain anyway, they'd probably sooner take on a young guy and show him the ropes than hire someone who was used to doing it the old way and teach him to adapt. Maybe it was more realistic for a man in my situation to look for a different job in a different business altogether, but one where I could make use of my experience from here, so it would take no time at all for me to acquaint myself with the newer aspects. I couldn't think of what line of work that would be, right off the top of my head, but that there had to be several, which, if not identical, were in some way related to ours, I was pretty sure about that. But how did you go about it, if you wanted to move into something else? Do you apply for positions while you've still got the one you have? Without telling anyone? Sneak off to job interviews in secret, without saying a word to your colleagues or your superiors, until you actually get the job and have a contract in your hand? Or was it best to lay all your cards on the table right from the start, let everyone, including the management, know that as of today I'm looking for a new position, and I'm going to take it, if I find it, and they offer it to me? Wouldn't that just serve to sour relations unnecessarily, no matter how short a time you may have left? Would it not, no matter how well intentioned it was . . . a man in the prime of life with significant work experience looking around for a new job . . . be perceived as a betrayal? And what if fate was so cruel that, after you'd already informed everybody that as of tomorrow I'm on the lookout for something new, you *found nothing* or worse still, *got none* of the positions you liked the look of and applied for?

A shrill reprimand from the livid bell over the metal clock woke me from my musings: I hadn't noticed time passing at all. As usual I waited until everybody was out before I went around and turned off all the machines. The silence was deafening. I stood over by the door for a while listening to their voices out in the changing room, Heljesen was busy telling the others about a distant relation on his mother's side who'd been through some dramatic experience, going into a rich variety of meticulous details in his squeaky, feminine voice. I thanked God it wasn't me that had to sit in there nodding and acting like I was interested. Then I switched off the light . . . and it was as if I'd waited as long as I could before doing so, because it was the last time I was going to do it . . . and went in to them. Most of them had their coats on already and were just standing exchanging some last words, bags in their hands, before going home. Without looking at anyone, I opened my locker, hung my dustcoat up inside, and released the net from my damp hair, running my hands through it a bit in order to air it. I have, like the others here, a narrow depression running the whole way around my head, which the elastic on the hairnet, from so many years of use, slips into by itself. Helene used to call it my halo.

We caught sight of her as soon as we came out, and I don't know, but it was as though each of us, as we slinked after one another across the yard, was hoping . . . although we all naturally tried to hide it as well as we could . . . that it was *us*, and not one of the others, that she was standing there waiting for, before one after another we drew close enough to establish that unfortunately it wasn't. I came last and by so doing expected that I would also be the last one to have this confirmed. But just as I was about to go past her, she let go of the gatepost, walked over to me, and stopped, almost as if she wanted to block my path. She was wearing a blue coat, had square glasses, and stood with her arms folded, trembling slightly. Had she been standing and waiting long? The guys who had their cars parked in the street took their time getting in, I noticed, whereas the others had probably already formed an opinion. I didn't know what to say; I thought I'd leave it up to her.

"Andreas," she said flatly, like a simple statement of fact. It was strange to hear my name like that, Helene never uses it. She attempted a smile, but her lips didn't obey, they only trembled, reinforcing her wretched appearance. Because she really looked wretched, like some ragged animal that didn't belong in the capital, who had come here with one particular purpose in mind, and even that only after having battled its natural inclinations, and it as though what really mattered to her was about getting it over with as quickly as possible, so that she could escape the city and go back home. I put my bag in my other hand and placed my free hand gently on her shoulder. She still kept her arms folded, as if she refused to let go of herself for fear of collapsing. And I escorted her like that, still without having said a word to her, to the café on the corner a few blocks away. I knew that it was the place where some of my colleagues usually had a beer after work, but be that as it may, the most important thing was to get this miserable creature inside before she froze in the posture she obviously insisted on retaining, anyway I only needed to take a quick look around in order to reassure myself that there wasn't a single familiar face in the place. Once inside, she just stood there, in the middle of the room, as if she had put her fate completely in my hands, as if she was still standing waiting as she had by the gate. I guided her onto a chair in a relatively quiet corner and asked her what she wanted, but she just shook her head, not because she didn't want something, but because she didn't care what she got . . . at least that's how I interpreted it.

She finally relaxed the unnatural hold she had on herself, placed both arms on the table and cupped the warm glass in her hands, her face was harried and drawn . . . I examined her . . . she looked like a sketch of herself, as though I'd attempted to draw her from memory, and every line, every stroke had been too coarse, a little too harsh. She drank her toddy without being aware of it, not looking at me or anything else in the room. I began to feel cold myself, and I regretted not having ordered the same. But she seemed to liven up a little now, she got some colour in her cheeks, and her shoulders slouched, whether that was because she'd relaxed, or, on the contrary, because she was exerting herself even further. Then the tears came, as expected I suppose. With her gaze still fixed on nothing, they just began to flow, first from one eye and then from the other: when she blinked a thick film covered both of them. Eventually she turned to face me and I felt it only reinforced my already deep-seated embarrassment, knowing that even if she stayed sitting like that staring at me for a good long time, I still wouldn't come up with anything sensible to say.

"What can I do?" she asked, in a voice that was surprisingly clear . . . despite the fact that she was still crying she must have realized that it was up to her to begin. And now that she'd made the effort to say something, it was as though she'd woken up and suddenly remembered why she'd come to see me. And then out it came, all at once: "Oh, what can I do, what can I do?" she chanted, again and again between crying fits. "Oh, Andreas, what *can* I do?" It was awkward; I had no idea of what you're supposed to say in situations like that. Besides, my sister and I have never been particularly close, and so I felt more than a little embarrassed that she should choose me of all people to confide in. Didn't she have countless friends back home who she could turn to? And as for Fredrik, I hardly knew anything about him, I'd only met him two or three times, first at the wedding and then at a few Christmas get-togethers since, so I felt far from able to offer an opinion on any qualifications he may have as a husband and father of three. But seeing how she'd come all this way, and it having been such a long time since we'd seen each other, I didn't feel like I could turn her away. There she sat, her whole face puffed up and wet, with her hand on my arm, rocking it gently back and forth, as if she was trying to wake me up too . . . a call to arms, I suppose, since I'd barely opened my mouth since we met and probably looked completely petrified sitting there, showing no sign of compassion or any of the other things she'd come to get.

And then I felt that I couldn't hold back any longer, and I began to babble while I held onto her arm, exactly the same way she'd held onto mine, it just gushed out of me . . . how you probably couldn't expect everything from a man . . . how lately I'd had to stop from forgetting that I myself am a father of two, two grown women, two proper people. "I simply don't understand it," I said. "On a few occasions when Helene's mentioned them, I've had to ask her who in the world she's talking about!" I exclaimed, with genuine amazement in my voice.

"Maybe it's not that strange when you think about it, they haven't been great at keeping in touch since they left home.

Besides, it's not something you can just demand of someone, that he goes around remembering he's a father all the time. Is it? Isn't that often the way it is though, that it's the things you are which, naturally enough, you also find easiest to forget?"

I looked at her, in the hope of assent.

"Anyway, what I would have said," I went on, still uncertain about how much of what I was saying was really getting through to her, "was that it's no joke, living together with three women for so many years, in a world that they make their own over time. They're barely out of diapers before they start with diapers all over again! It was fine to start off with. They were easy to fool, and I soon figured out that if I alternated in a meticulous way between offering tempting rewards on the one hand and being mercilessly strict on the other then I could get them to do pretty much anything, as long as I was careful about choosing the right method at the right time, based upon a careful evaluation of each particular situation. I could really see it quite clearly, a little too much of the first and they became blasé, but if I overdid it the other way then they turned tough as nails and paid me back in my own coin. Little did I know, back then, that although I'd gained the upper hand, it wouldn't last long beyond those happy, early years. And that once you lose the upper hand, you get all that manoeuvring and manipulation you yourself have utilized back in your face, only ten times worse. And all with one essential difference, that I, as opposed to them, wasn't able to look forward to the prospect of everything turning to my advantage in a few years. I just had to bite the bullet and accept that they were superior to me, completely superior, both of them, that they had me in the palms of their hands, wrapped around their little fingers, simple as that. And what was I supposed to say, I who out of love and consideration alone had gambled everything, only to lose it all? Let alone what was I supposed to *do*? The only choice you've got, in my experience anyway, is to take care of the good memories you're left with. To immerse yourself in them, yes, it was like holding up a crucifix to vampires when they came stumping along at all hours, white-faced, dark shadows under their eyes, with long nails and red lips. Believe me, it's an awful sight, seeing someone, never mind your own daughters, once so helpless they screamed at the top of their voices if Helene or I so much as left the room for a second or two, grow up to be like that. Marit in particular was really horrible for a while, finagled her way in, showered me with affection, was charming and funny, in a way she knew I'd fall for, when there was something she wanted, and as soon as she got it she'd make faces behind my back, I saw her reflected in the window once, when I turned around. Duplicitous in every respect, but gifted at it, Good God, how gifted!"

I gulped down the rest of the coffee in one go, I'd been talking so fast I'd almost been slurring my words.

"Besides, there's something about that apartment of ours," I said, "there's no evidence there that anyone ever grew up between its walls, that there were ever children toddling around in there, pulling books off the shelves and spilling jam on the carpets. There's been too much cleared away and changed around since then. Although, I have to admit, I'm completely unable to picture those rooms any other way than they look right now. Everything seems so old and ingrained the way it is, as if the whole place, the entire apartment, the entire building for that matter, would collapse if I so much as went over to the corner table in the living room and removed the wrought-iron candlestick that's standing on it. I can't get my head around the fact that it once looked very different, as far as I remember it hasn't been refurnished once in all the years we've lived there. So where did we put Marit and Nina when they were small . . . well, you know, I really couldn't tell you. I can't remember us having a nursery, either. If we did have one I really can't imagine where it would have been. It's not a big place either, I mean there's just about enough space for the two of us, along with all of our things, not that we've acquired all that many in the last few years. The only thing I can think of offhand is that we replaced the old television set with one that was more up-to-date. Apart from that there haven't been any renovations or refurbishment, I can promise you that. And I've seen how much space children take up when they're at a certain age, and especially if there's more than one, because it's not only the children you need to think about, well, you know all about it yourself, they insist on having piles of toys and every kind of gadget in the world in order to satisfy their so-called needs, if you have children these days and the inside of your house doesn't look like an amusement park then you run the risk of being accused of parental negligence, that's the impression I get. And slap bang in the middle of all this, respectable adults gladly live out the best years of their lives without thinking of anything other than how to make sure their snot-nosed kids get the best out of life, every single day, year after year. When I go from room to room and look around with that in mind, it seems utterly unbelievable that something like that could have gone on in our home. There's not one picture, not so much as a little drawing even, that bears witness to it. It's just the two of us there. Me. And Helene. So it's like I say, sister of mine. It's just the two of us there."

She calmed down after that, I bought her a glass of wine and we chatted for an hour or so before she had to leave in order to catch the afternoon train back home. I offered to walk her to the station but she declined, and was quite firm in her refusal. I couldn't help, when she'd gone, but wonder if I had hurt her . . . or maybe she felt that I'd insulted her . . . I know how easy it is to come off like you're lecturing other parents when your own children are older than theirs. In any case, there was something infinitely sad about that figure in its blue coat setting out for home . . . I stood on the corner outside the café watching her . . . and it suddenly struck me that she couldn't possibly know how to get from here to the central station . . . and that there was something unnatural, yes, almost perilous about the way she set out, swift and purposeful, as if she knew the city inside out.

I didn't quite know what to do. I was already late . . . maybe I should call to let Helene know . . . ? either that I was on my way, in order to put her mind at rest . . . or that I'd be held up until later still . . . which would also put her mind at rest. Out of habit I walked in the direction of the square . . . but not to the tram stop, where I'd usually go, rather to a phone box a little farther on, on a corner by the cathedral. I had to look in the phone book, I realized I didn't know the number . . . was it really the first time I was going to punch it in myself? And for a moment I felt a ticklish anticipation at the thought of Helene's disconcerted voice on the other end. But as I remained standing there with my index finger poised on the first of the sticky keys, the humming of the dial tone in my ear made me think of the factory . . . it was as though I was standing outside listening to the machines through the wall . . . If a taxi drives by the department store next, I said to myself, then I'll call . . . if not, I won't. Right after that a tram went rumbling by, like a multi-coloured fun-fair ride, like a float in a parade. Slightly taken aback, I hung the receiver back in place . . . I must have taken it for granted that it was a taxi that would come.

I walked up toward the post office, filling my lungs with a dose of August's most optimistic oxygen. A month, maybe less, until I had to get my gloves out again. For me it's a pleasure to start wearing that heavy coat every autumn, it's always felt natural to me to put something on when going out the door, it's not right to just move from one place to the other willy-nilly, as if it didn't make any difference whether you were indoors by yourself or outside among people. But that's the way everyone behaves in summer, as if they feel at home everywhere. Walk around the supermarket barefoot and in shorts. Openly breastfeed their screaming brats on the tram. Eat chicken on a bench in the middle of the city. Once I saw someone sitting clipping their nails, *their toenails*, under the statue of Wergeland on Students' Promenade! I decided not to say anything to the woman behind the counter, not so much as a thank you, as she counted out my money for me. The bank notes felt like they were swelling up in my inside pocket, I was aware of a mild pressure on one side of my chest and felt like a criminal as I went out, I was just waiting for someone to shout STOP THIEF!

I thought: For the next twelve hours I can do whatever I want . . . whatever good that is . . .

In a large display window with brass instruments . . . all the brightly polished horns, trumpets, and note stands shone so brightly, twinkling like a thousand little candles, that I just *had* to stop and look . . . I caught sight of myself, bent over slightly and with my bag in my hand. The first thing that struck me was that this was a man of indeterminate age, that if someone who didn't know me had seen me now it would be impossible for them to guess what age I was. I could be old, I could be young. This cheered me up. And not only that . . . I thought . . . it would probably be impossible for this outsider, this stranger, to guess what kind of person I was, how I usually conducted myself, what sort of mood I was generally in, if I was the calm or quick-tempered type, what type of job I had, if I had a family or not, how I would react to being approached, in short, *what kind of person I was.* This depressed me. If it wasn't apparent, to some degree at least, on the surface, what kind of person I was, then what must people think of me, on the tram everyday to and from work for example, there was always a familiar face there, not that I'd ever said hello to them, but they took the same route as me every single day of the year. I'd even made up some background stories about them. And they hadn't all been flattering, that's for sure. Well, at least the books were balanced to some degree, then. But what was so disheartening, perhaps, was seeing, in the greenish-brown reflection of the window, how lacking in character I looked, so completely without personality, so utterly devoid of the pronounced features that you usually associate with strong personalities, people with an interest in one thing or another, people who are passionate about something, are absorbed in something, who've lived through a crisis and been marked by it, who've had unusual experiences that have made them stronger, who've travelled a lot, who've read a lot, who know a lot, who have lots of opinions. Perhaps that feeling of dejection was only reinforced, who knows, by all the splendour of the display window, all that sparkling brass standing there, reminding me of fêtes and festivities. I wouldn't be the slightest bit surprised, I thought, if the face in the mirror . . . window, I mean . . . slowly began to change, now while I stood looking, that it slowly changed and became that of another. And I felt pretty sure that this new face, no matter what it ended up looking like, would leave me with exactly the same feeling as the one I stood looking at now. I squeezed my eyes shut and was about to lean in closer in order to try it out when I banged my forehead against the glass with a thud: startled, I recoiled and looked around quickly to see if anyone was watching. The window in front of me shook, or *swayed* is perhaps closer to the truth, because the surface was enormous . . . the window measured maybe three or four metres across . . . which made the reflection billow back and forth, before it eventually gave way to a shudder, quivering like that for a long time, as if it would never settle down.

I waited until the worst of the pain had gone before walking on. Was I worried it was visible? I didn't know where I was going. I couldn't go home, not for a while anyway. I'd go someplace and eat. Find a restaurant that wasn't too expensive, maybe buy a paper on the way. I didn't know where people went, or where it was good to go. What must Helene think, now that she'd been left on her own all evening without so much as a word? I saw the tram coming and for a moment I considered running to catch it, getting on and letting it carry me home, getting in and spinning Helene some yarn and spending the evening as usual. Then it occurred to me that, in all likelihood, she'd be in a bad mood with me no matter what time of the evening I got home, and that I may as well put it off for a few more hours, seeing as I had the chance.

I went into one of the oldest pubs in the city, ordered the special, and a beer, a pilsner, a large pilsner. The beer arrived first. They'd rather keep you waiting, I thought, so you drink it up out of sheer boredom and then have to buy another when the food finally comes. I took a big mouthful, it felt good. Above my head there hung a landscape painting that had seen better days. Beside that a framed letter, the paper yellow with age and the handwriting illegible. Whoever wrote it must have been relatively well known, I thought, famous enough to have his letter mounted and framed, but not famous enough for it to end up in a museum. There were also two pictures of racing cars from the '20s or '30s hanging beside each other, they looked like those little handheld vacuum cleaners you see attached to the wall in kitchens, the first was a photograph, the other a painting . . . or were they both paintings? . . . it was hard to tell. On the table in the corner there stood a three-branched candlestick with two candles in it, it looked like a cripple.

I'd gotten halfway through my drink when I suddenly felt the need . . . or the *obligation*, rather . . . to do something grand, something completely unexpected . . . outrageous if need be . . . make a splash . . . whatever the cost. I just didn't know what it could be. For a moment I considered ringing up Jens Olav and squaring things with him, he should be home around now, if nothing else we could exchange a few words, to set my mind at rest. But I'd just have to be patient and wait until tomorrow, do it then, in between shifts. If I was to call him at home, and it would be the very first time, then I'd probably only contribute to the drama, blow it up into something bigger than it was, seeing as I found it necessary to disturb his domestic peace in order to clear the matter up. But was there actually anything to clear up? Truth be told, there wasn't any *matter* to speak of. But there would be, if I called. If the next person who goes by the window has a hat on I'll make the call, I thought, if not I won't.

Since he lost his wife, his house, and everything he owned in a fire, Jens-Olav has had this look about him, brows knitted, gimlet-eyed, which makes every slightest error any of the rest of us commit in our work seem like an outright crime. Any friendliness he shows is full of insinuation: if he picks something up off the floor for one of us then his expression is one of indignation that we could have been so careless as to drop it. But perhaps you couldn't begrudge him this, all things considered.

Two young man flashed past the window on bikes, neither of them had a hat on. I breathed a sigh of relief, although at the same time I felt unsettled for putting so much faith in my immediate surroundings.

I tried to imagine what it looked like at Jens-Olav's place. I could picture him, on his own, opening up the door into a hallway with nothing but a wardrobe and a few jackets hanging in it, taking off his coat, going into the kitchen, turning on the radio, sitting down at the table, flicking through the newspaper, staring out over the grey city, taking a burger or some frozen fish out of the fridge, turning on the hotplate, getting out the frying pan and banging it down, cutting off a knob of butter and scraping it off into the pan, sighing heavily while he waits for the heat to melt it. I didn't know if it was compassion or envy I felt most. Grief like that . . . I couldn't manage to think of it as anything other than liberation, liberation from all the trivial things that otherwise have such power over you. All the niggling concerns that prey on your mind and that never stop knocking you off course because none of them are big enough to sweep the other problems aside. No, it was hard to get away from the fact that there was something enticing about it, losing your wife and everything you owned in a flash, no matter how dreadful it was . . . to be visited by some great sorrow on which to concentrate your emotions instead of continuing to torment yourself with thousands of small ones. *Scorched from the surface of the earth as if they'd never been . . .*

The food arrived. But something wasn't quite right about the sight of the plate sitting there steaming in front of me, and I couldn't bring myself to eat before I figured out what is was. Then I realized. *There was nobody sitting on the other side of my table.* I was on my own. I was out, on my own, and about to eat. People don't do that, anyway I'd never done it before. It was all right to have a coffee or a beer on your own, but not to eat. Eating out is something you do together with other people, on special occasions, if you have something to celebrate, or if you're treating yourself to a night on the town, going to the theatre or the movies and having a bite to eat afterward, Helene and I, along with Elise and Hans-Jacob, used to do it a lot at the beginning, in the first few years of our marriage. But I'd never sat at a restaurant table alone and been waited upon. It didn't feel natural, no, not in the slightest. I felt it went against something on a very profound level, I noticed that now. But it was too late, the steam was already rising up into my face. At the same time I experienced a sort of anticipatory thrill as I lifted my fork and was about to begin, like the feeling you get when you do something for the first time, something not quite within the limits of the law, well, your own laws, if nothing else. I took the first tentative bite and chewed carefully. Nothing on the plate was heated properly, not even the gravy, and to my great surprise, and subsequent thrill, this thoroughly prevalent tepidity only served to give the meal an added tang, as though it carried the taste aloft in triumph! It tasted simply wonderful. Yes, I became aware, bite after bite, how the situation was transforming itself from being unnatural and uncomfortable into more and more of a delight . . . the pleasure and enjoyment grew, as if this lukewarm meal, which went against my deepest principles, was turning out to be the best I'd ever eaten. *It was as though I was sitting there eating my own inhibitions.* And it was all gone in less than a quarter of an hour! Five flatbreads; I ate them all, and used the last one to wipe the last of the gravy off my plate. Poor Helene. No, not poor Helene. It wasn't a pity about her. It wasn't a pity about anyone. Everyone had to manage as best he, or she, could.

But I'm no big fan of the theatre, I thought, at that reminder of our youthful escapades. Those times we were at the theatre I just sat there with an intense desire for the performance to end. The ending was the only thing I took any pleasure in, when I realized that things were coming to a close: the summing up and rounding off . . . the winding up of all the threads, is that a good way to put it? . . . but halfway through the play . . . or God forbid, during the opening scenes, the first fifteen minutes, I just sat there with a crushing feeling that nothing was moving, that time was standing still, that I'd be stuck in that seat until the day I died. It was the opposite with movies, though . . . the longer they lasted and the more time there was until a resolution to their problems the more I enjoyed them, yes, I even enjoyed the beginning, the very first minutes, as though it was a little film in itself. And was almost in a rage . . . although I never showed it, of course . . . if I missed the start of a film on television, which, after a while, turned out to be really good. Yes, I was willing to see the first hour and more as one long preamble for what was to come, a gradual, joyful build-up. But when it started to near the end, move toward a clearing-up of all the confusion . . . which was generally pretty banal in comparison with the splendid complexity of the initial mystery or conflict . . . then I usually grew despondent and yearned for the glorious uncertainty and tingling anticipation of that first hour. Come to think of it, how long had it been since I'd seen a film I thought was really good? I took a few big gulps, I felt the beer making me drowsy . . . I enjoyed it. It was like my head alone was tired, that it was in need of some relaxation. And it dawned on me that I really didn't like the way things grew out of all proportion as soon as you put them into words, even when you just sat the way I was now, quietly, all by yourself, and thought some things about it. Even the smallest things expanded between your fingers, as though you couldn't help thinking about it . . . thinking about *anything*. . . without blowing it up into something far too big and grotesque.

The waitress cleared the table and lit the tea candle, as if to say: I hope you sit here a little while longer. A fat man with long, grey hair sat two tables away and fiddled incessantly with a cigarette that he smoked with little nervous puffs, while at the same time he jerked one foot at regular intervals, as though something had stung or bitten him. His face could have been a woman's, I saw it as he turned around, he had a long nose that resembled a carrot which had gone old and soft. He had a peaked cap pulled tightly down over his grey wisps of hair, an army cap with a camouflage pattern that made it look like a stone. Suddenly he slammed his hand down hard on his table, as if trying to hit a fly. I thought of Didriksen. Flies are scavengers, he once confided to me. If you have difficulty getting the better of them, the best thing you can do, instead of running around after them, is to take up a position calmly at a spot where you've recently killed one, because sooner or later they'll make their way over to their old friends. If you stand patiently in position, with a bit of luck you can eradicate an entire swarm without needing to move. And as if that wasn't enough he had to crush them flat with his bag afterward as well. You need to hear a crunch, he once said. When you hear it *crunching*, then it's over.

Bang! He tried to hit a new one, the grey-haired guy. He smoked nervously and took such tiny sips of his beer that, from the look of his glass, it didn't seem like he'd drank anything. I found myself waiting for him to turn around and explain to me what was going on, why he was so nervous. That he was sick perhaps, or unemployed, or a drug addict. And then he did turn around . . . right around . . . and looked at me, a piercing stare, which caught me completely off guard, given the rest of his appearance . . . it was as if he'd noticed me studying him and forming an opinion about him. And there was . . . there was a *power* in his eyes that took me by surprise. The power . . . I thought, once I'd managed to compose myself, and the grey-haired man was once again absorbed in his own broodings . . . *the power in the eyes of a man who has given up on everything* . . . at least that was what I thought I'd seen in them . . . one who has nothing left to lose . . . who has no interest in the workings of the world . . . and so takes people for what they are, not for what he *wants them to be* . . . a look so pure and hard and clear that I felt it in the pit of my stomach. Inferior, I felt completely inferior . . . as if he was looking *right through me* . . . as if I wasn't capable of concealing anything from this man . . . nor was there any point in pretence or in putting on a friendly face. And this grey-haired bum, sitting there farting in public, had become a person that I was anxious to make a good impression on, all of a sudden, like some higher authority you need to appease. It was important to me now that this grey-haired . . . *loser*, as I'd first called him, in my offhand eagerness to label people . . . as if it was that quality itself which had made him turn around . . . that this grey-haired man *didn't* see through me, that he wouldn't be left with the impression that I was a son of a bitch. I was afraid of him, I felt like a hypocrite. I cursed the ironic coincidence that had put me beside him in a place that, when I had come in, had had countless unoccupied tables. If he approached me, I would have broken down, I was sure of it, I would have babbled away like a lunatic, revealed myself to the whole world. I felt damned, convinced that I didn't have a chance of making it out here, outside the protective walls of home, out here in the real world, among real people. It was as if I had based my entire life on the kindness and consideration I could derive from my immediate surroundings, which comfort I now had to accept no longer existed. I felt like a fool, like someone whose development has been at a standstill since his youth and has never been corrected, who's never been made aware of the grotesque disparity between reality and his perception of reality. My views are of no importance, I thought: of absolutely no importance. No one who hears them takes them seriously. Anyone who wants to can take me on without any difficulty, get the better of me, reject every assertion I might make. In any case, resistance would be minimal, laughable almost.

A bit of food, a moist scrap, had gotten stuck to the bottom of my beer, I saw it magnified in its golden unreality through the bottom of the glass every time I took a gulp, and every time it felt like it had gotten into my mouth and I'd swallowed it. I raised the glass and picked it off, it stuck to my fingertip and I looked around in vain for somewhere to get rid of it, but no suitable edges . . . in the end I had to rub it off onto the tablecloth, discreetly.

Not a moment too soon, because the waitress came back over to ask me if I'd like anything else, coffee or another beer? Two large breasts heaved behind her apron, and this filled me with delight, brightened things up after the gloomy influence of the grey-haired man. I felt the warmth from her as she bent over the table to clear it off. She smiled, *showed me such kindness that it was almost hard to bear,* and for no other reason than I was probably one of hundreds of customers in the course of a day. I could see how busy she was, careening like a ship between the tables, now with glasses, now with plates, rarely empty-handed, and then with her hands thrust deeply in the ample pocket of her apron, and I almost felt a pang of jealousy as she leaned over another table, occupied by four rough-looking characters, and laughed heartily at some remarks, obviously aimed at her, and which were anything but discreet, judging by the roars of laughter coming from the louts afterward. Why did I feel like we had an understanding? Unfounded, perhaps? We were far from having anything in common . . . we were too different for that, me and the waitress with hair that looked like a wreath of thorns . . . but I suddenly got the idea that she was able to interpret my every little nuance, and not only that, but to interpret them correctly, as easily as making out the line of my brow or a particular feature of my mouth. There was a friendliness in her eyes that told me so, or inspired me to believe it was so. Did that also mean that I felt superior to her? That I, unconsciously, and based upon the waitress-guest relationship that existed between us, almost took for granted that a corresponding one held sway as well . . . only on a deeper level, which, when I thought about it, I had no interest in cultivating? I didn't want to be superior to her. I didn't want to be superior to anyone. But I couldn't rid myself of the feeling that if I now took advantage of this relationship of trust I thought existed, by confiding in her for example . . . something I had in no way considered doing, which, come to think of it, rendered the problem quite hypothetical . . . too hypothetical to be taken seriously? . . . it would have meant that I'd be exploiting her, abusing her trust, undeserving of her open mind. Didn't this very understanding on her part, this open and free and easy contact between us, have the most value to me if

I *didn't* take advantage of it? And then I wouldn't risk being disappointed either, if I was proved incorrect.

Now she was standing at my table again with her lemon-scented cloth in her hand. I considered that I ought to be wary of saying something now that might insult her and in so doing sever what little understanding we had reached. "Could I get . . ." I said and didn't manage to say anything more before a new smile spread across her face, warmer now, if possible, as if she understood more than she was willing to express . . . out here anyway . . . and she disappeared once more through the green swing door with a tray full of empty glasses she'd collected in the meantime. Of course it could have been me who, without being aware of it, had signalled with my hand or my eyes and immediately put her on the right track, told her what I was going to request. My hope was that she'd soon sweep through the doors again, like I'd seen her do several times already. I stared at the door as it groaned and came slowly to rest . . . it almost had something mystical about it now, I thought, like the entrance to a grotto or a temple.

In order to kill time while I was waiting, I don't know why really, I looked over at the grey-haired man again. Now he seemed completely harmless, yes, comical more than anything else, a lost soul, in a world that must appear to him to be more loathsome the more normal the people around him were, or gave the impression of being. He turned around but didn't look at me, and it wouldn't have mattered anyway, because now his eyes were blurry and dim . . . had what I'd seen a little while ago been some sort of last-gasp effort? . . . there was no life left in his eyes now, they looked like cobwebs had grown over them, like there was a spider lying in wait in each one.

I was startled by the sudden arrival of the waitress. She put the bill down in front of me, pressed it down brazenly with her thumb, then turned her back to take an order from a nearby table. I liked that, her leaving me alone to sort out the money thing. There's something vulgar about counting money while they stand there waiting . . . nobody, in my opinion, can manage to do it without seeming like a tightwad. Speaking of which, it had been so long since I'd eaten out that I didn't know how much was considered a reasonable tip. It's always bugged me, the whole tipping thing, you're out having a good time and then you're expected to fork out even more after you've paid for everything. Which has usually cost more than enough as it is. And then you're left with a bad feeling at the end of it all, whether you do one thing or the other, leave too big a tip and feel like you've been swindled or leave too little and know you'll be seen as a skinflint. This day however, was so special that I knew exactly what I was going to do, I'd leave an extra thirty kroners, so that when I was leaving I could give a magnanimous wave of my hand to let her know that the additional amount, that was for her, all of it.

I was on my way out when I heard her shout out after me, I turned around and sure enough, it was her, still standing over at my table and motioning with both hands, as if she was helping a car back out of a driveway. I had no choice but to go over to her, what with all the commotion she was making. She kept signalling with her hands until I was right beside her, as if she was afraid I'd disappear in another direction as soon as she stopped.

"Is there something wrong?" I asked, making an effort to seem friendly.

She didn't say anything, merely pointed down at the saucer. I got a shock when I looked down, at first glance it looked like there was only a single note there, with the coins on top as ballast. I shook them off and picking it up, rubbed at little at one corner so that the other note, which for some reason or another had gotten stuck onto the first, unfolded like a wing. I felt like a magician as I handed her the notes. The waitress slapped herself on the forehead in an expression of self-reproach. I smiled and said it was fine.

"I didn't mean to . . ." she began to say.

"I know," I said. "I know."

"It's been nonstop all day," she apologized. "People are coming and going the whole time, and we have to keep an eye on everything at once."

I nodded and said that I could see that it was hard going, the way they had to keep at it from early until late.

"People don't know what it's like," she said. "Most customers don't see beyond their own tables, they think they're the only ones we have to look after while they're here. They take exception to the slightest oversight or mistake, without taking into consideration that at the same time as we're bending over backwards to cater for them, we're bending over backwards for another ten or fifteen people as well."

I tried, as best as I could, since I was standing with my bag in my hand and so giving every indication of being on my way, to express my great understanding of the difficulties she faced on a daily basis in a demanding job. But it was clear to me that she had no intention of letting me go just yet, on the contrary, to my dismay, she edged back onto the corner of the table so that she was half-standing, half-sitting. "Sometimes I feel like putting my foot down," she said. "Throw everything over and just level with them, grab them by the collar and drag them into the kitchen so they can take a look for themselves. Some of them can be so unbelievably arrogant, they think they own the whole world, they think that's what nature intended, for us to dance in attendance on them and be at their beck and call. It's enough to make you sick. Just because they're paying they think they can demand anything at all."

I glanced over at the exit but looked away when I noticed she was staring at me.

"You know, there're people who actually snap their fingers when they want to attract our attention." She put her cleaning cloth on the table and pressed her fists against her hips. "They snap their fingers. Like this." Then she snapped her fingers, as if she thought I didn't know what it meant. "But you know what, when they do that I just stay right where I am, I don't budge from the spot. You have to draw the line somewhere. No way am I going to obey orders like that. I might be a waitress, but I'm not a dog. I'm not going to trot over to someone sitting there snapping their fingers. What would be next if we put up with that kind of thing? I'll tell you. Next they'd start whistling at us. Believe me." She whistled, loud and shrill. "In the end there wouldn't be any difference between a customer in a café and a dog trainer, other than the collar and the dog biscuits."

I couldn't do anything but say that I agreed, but at the same time I made sure to look at the clock in such an exaggerated way that she'd have had to be blind not to understand that I really needed to get going.

But she continued. "No, like I said, I'd like to really give a couple of them the works someday, set an example, once and for all, then maybe the next time some of them might think twice before treating another working person like an inferior. I'd drag them by the hair into the kitchen, that's right, and show them the kind of conditions we work in. Then each and every one of them would be a little less cocky. Do you want to come in and take a look?" She leaned forward and for a moment I thought she was planning to make good on her threats, grab me by the collar and drag me away with her. "Come on, I'll show you what we have to put up with if we want to keep our jobs. Maybe you think we've all kinds of amenities back there? A break room, a smoking room, a changing room . . . well? Is that how you picture it when you see us sailing out of there with a plate on each finger? Come and have a look, come on, then your curiosity will be satisfied. Then you won't wonder about it the next time you come here and start demanding things."

There was something aggressive about her now that I didn't like, I really have to get away from her as soon as possible, I thought, but in some strange way she managed to hold me captive with her indefatigable nagging, I don't know why but I couldn't manage to tear myself away.

"How did you picture it, when you were sitting here? Well? Do you think it's like the royal palace in there? Is that what you think?"

She leaned even further forward and got hold of my coat collar.

"What is it you actually think we're like? I'd really like to know, because then I could see about setting you straight about whatever ideas you have. Good and straight. What did you think it'd be like, can you answer me that, when you sat here earlier shovelling food into your mouth, anyone would think you hadn't had a proper meal in weeks. What's wrong with you? Do you think we hike our skirts up and pull our knickers down every time we disappear in there? Is that what you think we're up to in there? That the chef is back giving us a good you-know-what between every order?"

At this point she took her dishcloth and waved it in front of my face, showering lemon droplets everywhere, as though she had to restrain herself to keep from slapping me with it. Then she jumped down from the table, put her face right up to mine, and hissed: "Get the fuck out into the world and take a look around, man, before you get any ideas about how people make do in life!"

I had hoped these would be her parting words, because she snatched the money from the saucer and was about to put it into the pocket of her apron, but she stopped briefly to count them, the surplus coins, surveyed them with a practiced glance and, to her bewilderment I suppose, ascertained that her guest, whom she'd so heedlessly overwhelmed with her accumulated resentment, had in fact left her a kindly tip, more than she had reason to expect, and more than she deserved now at any rate. And now my generosity was rewarded. I saw how she turned positively radiant as she stood there in front of me, and I only just managed to turn, in order to leave, before she called out to me a second time, so that I had to turn around yet again, though I waited a little before I did it . . . I took another step toward the door first to make it look like I hadn't understood right away that it was me she meant.

"Thank you so much!" she said, but it was quite superfluous, the expression of gratitude in her face said more than any words could. She stood with the coins in her hand in front of her.

I nodded and smiled and was about to leave but she bounded over and grabbed me by the arm. "No, wait," she said. "Don't go. I'm sorry about what I said. I was wrong about you. Please, don't go. You're so kind. I just didn't see it right away. I let my feelings run away with me. I'm sorry. But it's so seldom that anyone cares. Even though it doesn't take very much." She was still holding the money up in front of her. "I mean, don't get me wrong, I don't mean that this isn't very much. My point was just that it's often so simple, the thing you could have done and which would have given so much pleasure, but all the same you don't do it, because you've got so many other things on your mind, so many worries of your own, but what do I know about the reasons. Do you know why it's suddenly become so rare for someone to take the time to make other people happy, even people they don't know, cast a little light into the darkness and gloom? It doesn't need to cost that much."

She stared deep into my eyes, as if she had caught sight of something in them.

"As you've just demonstrated," she said. Then she took me by the hand and said: "Oh hon, how could I have been so wrong about you?"

She squeezed hard on my wedding ring, making me wince.

"Oh, I'm sorry," she said, drawing my hand to her. "Oh, I'm sorry," she said again and took careful hold of my ring finger, lifting it up to study it more closely, and turning it this way and that in order to look at it from every angle.

"You poor thing," she said, and it was obvious that she now felt she had to do something to make up for it. "Come with me."

She took a firm hold of my wrist and pulled me along after her. Before I knew it she'd hauled me up the stairs and pushed me through the green door, and all of a sudden I found myself in the back room, the door flapped behind us, fanning in the smell of greasy food. The room was tiny, yet it was full of people. An old woman grated carrots. A young boy washed glasses and plates. A man in chequered trousers and a white apron stood bent over a whole colony of hot-plates . . . he glanced over his shoulder when we came in, then he dipped a ladle into one of the pots and asked if I'd like to taste. I patted myself on the stomach and politely declined. He seemed to take offence at this, because he just stood there with the ladle in his hand as if he couldn't quite understand that I'd refused his offer, while dark, heavy drops gathered under its bowl and hit the floor with a steady rhythm. Meanwhile the waitress had gone over to one corner and started moving some empty cardboard boxes aside; after a while a low door came into view. There was a girl sitting in front of it wearing the same black-and-white outfit as the waitress and she was squeezing the last remains of tobacco out of a meagre cigarette butt while she held an ashtray up in front of her in her other hand, as though it was some precious piece of jewellery. The waitress . . . it was starting to annoy me that I didn't know her name . . . motioned to me and poked her friend with the tip of her shoe to get her to move. Then she opened the door and signalled for me to enter, or at least to come closer so I could take a look inside.

"Have a look," she said. "Have a look at the kind of conditions we live in."

I felt nauseated as I craned my neck and was about to take a look, as though afraid of being faced with an utterly revolting sight inside the little chamber. But it wasn't as bad as I'd thought . . . it certainly didn't look like it had been washed in there for several years, but there was a lightbulb in the lamp, a rubber mat for a blanket, and there were pictures from old magazines on the walls, which likely concealed the most merciless encroachments of time. There was no proper toilet there, just a round hole in the floor, a drain almost, with a platform running along each side, covered in boot marks. A young girl was sitting crouched at the other end of the room, which is to say, the room was just about large enough for one more of them in the same position to fit in there. I don't know what got into me, but for a moment I was sure this was the young girl who was missing, that she hadn't been kidnapped, that on the contrary she'd left home of her own free will in order to live and work together with her friends at the café. She glanced up at me briefly before continuing with whatever she was doing, and I had to stick my head in even further in order to see what it was: she was sitting reading an article from one of the magazine clippings.

I trusted that this was to be considered the highlight of the tour and wanted to avail myself of the opportunity to take my leave and withdraw discreetly. But this was obviously out of the question: the waitress grabbed me by the hand again . . . carefully this time, so as not to squeeze too hard . . . and firmly led me deeper into the premises, past the little lavatory and under a curtain that I had thought concealed a shelf, or a wall, but which turned out to be the entrance to a new room, an extremely large one, judging by my first glance, with walls at all kinds of angles, a staircase leading directly into one of them, where it was possible to make out the outline of a door that had been there, a swollen shadow in the wallpaper. There was an old man sitting at the end of a long table eating soup, wolfing it down as if he'd been given a deadline by which to complete his meal, and the slurping and sucking made an awful racket. A woman stood behind him supervising the meal . . . at least that's what it looked like, because she never took her eyes off him, she hadn't even looked up when the waitress and I came up from under the curtain, they seemed completely absorbed in their tasks, both her and the old man . . . the soup bowl spun like a coin on the table from the relentless motion of the spoon.

Then I saw something moving over by a stove that towered against the wall behind them. It looked like a large, dark larva in the dim light. As I got closer I saw that it was a person lying on a mattress on the floor, wrapped up in one, or perhaps several woollen blankets, his whole body lying there like a tightly bound bundle. A head stuck out from one end of the bundle, the head of a man around the same age as me. His forehead shone in the glow of the grille. He had it wiped at regular intervals by a small boy sitting on a stool in front of the oven: he alternated between doing that and throwing on more firewood in order to keep the heat up.

"Is he sick?" I asked the waitress, but she only shushed me, apparently the man on the mattress wasn't to be disturbed under any circumstances. We crept past . . . I instinctively followed my escort . . . and ended up in the farthest corner of the room where, inserted in the wall, there was a shelf, so low down that we had to bend over in order to see what was on it. But what I had thought was a shelf turned out to be the frame around a photograph, which had obviously wound up there only because there'd been a hook screwed into the wall from some earlier usage of the spot, I had difficulty seeing any other explanation for the peculiar placement: if you didn't know about the picture, it would be almost impossible to spot it. The waitress pointed at the picture . . . a little girl stood on some rocks by the shore with the ocean in the background . . . she drew a handful of jet-black hair away from her face and smiled bashfully . . . but also proudly . . . at the photographer who'd probably instructed her, told her how to stand . . . I understood from the smile of the waitress who it was. We remained standing like that for a while, with our backs bent, right up until the waitress straightened up with a loud groan. She didn't look at me . . . it seemed as if she was disappointed . . . maybe she'd counted on me saying something, or expected a particular reaction after I saw the picture? Her expression changed to one of introspection, which made it quite impossible to guess what she was thinking. I apologized, said that I appreciated being shown around and taking part in her world, but that it wasn't possible for me to be there any longer, I said that I had an appointment in town which I was already late for and which was of the utmost importance for me to keep. She didn't say anything, but she didn't look happy. And now it was her silence that held me back: I couldn't bring myself to leave before she said something that could be understood as an acknowledgment that I was now taking my leave of her.

I pointed at my watch, shrugged my shoulders, and threw my arms out in an expression of regret, my bag swung out and hit something standing on the pedestal beside me and this something fell to the floor, but didn't break, as far as I could hear. The waitress bent down and picked it up, then remained standing with it in her hand . . . I still couldn't quite make out what it was . . . as if it gave her another reason not to release me, not yet, not before I'd endured even more of these gloomy back rooms full of people who . . . it would seem . . . never set foot outside them.

"Yes, well," I said and gestured with my arms again, more carefully this time, she still stood patting the knick-knack as if it was a pet . . . and I continued to thank her for her kindness as I backed toward the curtain as quickly as I dared for fear of bumping into something else. Finally I felt the weight of the curtain against my back, I crouched down under it and hurried through the kitchen, the heat hit me, a reeking steam from the thousands of meals that must have been prepared there over the years. The man in the chequered trousers still stood there stirring. He turned as I went past, and once again he held the ladle up for me to have a taste, but I didn't dare to, no, I simply didn't dare to, he looked like the type who might put something disgusting in the customers' food purely for his own amusement. I had planned to leave the same way as I came in but caught sight of a door over by the sinks that offered me hope of going directly out into the chilly autumn air. As luck would have it, it turned out to be unlocked . . . it was only afterward that I thought about how much more likely it was *not* to have been . . . but to my disappointment I wasn't standing outside behind the restaurant, as I'd expected, but inside a closet, or at least that's what I thought at first, because as I hurried to close the door behind me everything went black. However, I didn't feel I could just turn around and go back, thereby admitting my blunder to that sly, con man of a cook, so I decided to explore the room before giving up and retreating. A thin shaft of light from a point on the wall went through the darkness like a wire. I bent forward and looked through the hole, and to my amazement I could see most of the café, I worked out that the peephole must be located around where the pictures of the racing cars hung. I turned and started to grope around, eventually putting my hand on something that felt like a hoop, I got a good grip and pushed, another door flew open, the cold air in my nostrils was liberating after that stodgy sauna of cabbage and gravy. The light caught me by surprise, it was as if that brief interval, in what I now under-stood had been the old kitchen entrance, had prepared me for the evening and the darkness, which was still only in its infancy.

It was a chilly autumn afternoon, and I think I smiled as I walked along. People looked at me. It was as if I could've, if I'd so wished, stopped any one of them and they would have stood there listen-ing, with rapt attention and genuine interest, to everything I had to say. I checked a few times to make sure I'd remembered to take my bag, because it just sort of hung there, weightless, in my hand, while at the same time I knew deep down that I would have discov-ered it right away if I'd left it somewhere, noticed immediately that it wasn't there. Was it because it had, as they say, *become a part of me?* I pondered this expression for a while, played with the words, tried to arrange them in a different order, just as a mathematician probably uses the time it takes him to get from one place to another to perform complicated calculations in his head, so that he gets in a little workout for his brain at the same time as the other kind of exercise. And then maybe he'd . . . and I chuckled at the thought . . .

get run over just before he was about to solve some difficult equation. While I, if I'd been run over now, would have left this earthly existence with my old satchel foremost in my mind.

Without really being aware of it, my pace had increased considerably after a few blocks, and I only now noticed this . . . I was hurrying along, for no reason whatsoever. So I forced myself, as soon as I became conscious of it, to walk more slowly, and eventually, after much effort, to stroll, or saunter, in an absent-minded sort of way. It required tremendous willpower to start with, I felt as though I was being strangled, I was walking with heavy chains around my ankles, in the middle of the multitude of busy professionals. I'd better pull myself together, I told myself in my sternest inner voice. There have to be limits. I succumb all too easily to setbacks, I always have a hard time remembering that if a shadow falls upon me, I can always just take a step to the side, into the sun. I told myself that there was no reason to be afraid of someone just because they wore an army cap. And I tried to convince myself that this impulsive escapade of mine out into the great outdoors . . . underhanded in nature, but be that as it may . . . was something I needed, something that would do me good, something that could inject some fresh blood into my veins, maybe grant me a fresh perspective on a few things. That's what you needed to do, I thought, so you don't stagnate entirely. You needed to break loose sometimes, and then you'd return to what was familiar with renewed vigour, a little more inspired, quite simply, than you would have been otherwise.

There was a man standing singing on a corner with a hat on the pavement in front of him, I got it into my head that it wasn't him, but another person, inside him, who sang every time, he, the one on the outside, opened his mouth. But hadn't I heard this melody before? Hadn't I walked past him several times? I looked around: The traffic was thinning out, the pedestrians were fewer, and the lights were coming on. The pace was different as well; people didn't walk with so much purpose as earlier, they weren't necessarily on their way from one place to another. I noticed a woman in a dark coat walking, very slowly, in my direction, and I thought that this was how, in a crowd, you could distinguish single people from those who were living with someone else, that the single people walk slowly, almost reluctantly. But wasn't that how I was walking myself, this evening? *Sauntering along . . .* without any particular goal. The thought depressed me. I felt that what I was doing now was at variance with everything I actually wanted to do, and I couldn't understand why I had put myself in such a situation of my own free will. I was confused and wasn't sure of anything save that it was only going to get worse if I continued to hang around this part of town. I'd even been so engrossed in my own thoughts that I'd paid no attention to where I was going . . . had perhaps walked back and forth past the same shops and the same cafés for over an hour, like a halfwit.

Helene's part in the whole thing, that's what annoyed me most. If only she'd been a little bit more understanding, a tiny bit easier to confide in, then with her help I could have shaken off this uneasiness, if in no other way than telling her everything, over dinner, everything that had happened at work that day, and how I felt about it all, and then if she'd told me in turn . . . *it wouldn't need to be more than a couple of sentences . . .* that of course things weren't the way I'd taken them . . . that of course it would all look different in the morning and everything would be back to normal . . . But instead I had to pull the wool over her eyes, act like a criminal, go underground, avoid my usual routes, hide in the crowd like a thief, and roam the city haphazardly for a entire afternoon and evening, just because I, unlike other, luckier men, could not go home and unburden myself to my wife.

As if my thoughts had directed my steps without my being aware of it, I was bewildered to find that I was standing facing a cinema placard: I'd stopped in front of it and stood studying it closely, the twisted facial expressions, the bright blue letters. I looked up at the shining colossi: CINEMA . . . the word itself had something menacing about it, not that I could explain why. A heavy door was the only thing that separated me from the box office, and even before it had managed to close again with its already familiar, it occurred to me, torturous moan, I had asked the lady in the grey shirt when the next screening began. Even though she must have known, she turned her head around and looked at a little board on the wall before she answered, I don't know if it was to impress me or if she did it out of habit.

"That long?" I asked, without thinking over whether this was a reasonable reaction. And it was obvious that I'd insulted her, because she narrowed her eyes and regarded me from then on with the greatest suspicion. Did she think I was out to make fun of her? In an attempt to pacify her, I don't know, I asked how much a ticket cost.

She only answered after a long pause, still with two small fiery knots in her eyes, as though, after careful consideration, she was attributing to me the worst possible motives for asking.

"Thanks," I said, "then I'd like a ticket please."

It was as if she couldn't believe her ears, nor did she seem to know what to do now, if she should serve me in the usual way or if she should wait and stay on her guard, in case I had something sneaky planned.

"Where would you like to sit?" she finally asked.

It had been so long since I'd been to the movies that it never entered my mind that you could choose. I felt like saying that it didn't matter, but at the same time I was afraid this would give her extra ammunition: "Somewhere in the middle," I said, not being able to think of anything better.

"Full," she said, almost before I'd finished speaking, finding it difficult to conceal the satisfaction it gave her.

"A little further back then," I said, and still she took a long time at the computer before she eventually gave me the tickets. I paid and went over and sat down on one of the red sofas, so flustered by this hostile encounter that I felt like I was sitting in a waiting room. But suddenly I was better disposed toward her. She's proud of her job, I thought, terribly proud, even though it's ever so small and insignificant. There was something heart-warming about the thought. But perhaps her pride is just a way to avoid despairing, I then thought, a way to keep from facing up to the problem, the knowledge of how small and insignificant it is, that job of hers.

In any case, I thought, those type of complications only ever arise over minor things . . . no one who was content with their work would dream of complicating purely formalized interactions . . . and I didn't know if that was a good or a bad thing. On a big screen in front of me they showed stills from coming attractions. I thought it was splendid to start off, but then I became aware of a sound coming from a black turret beside me, the distinctive sound of a projector changing slides, and then suddenly it all just seemed amateurish and common.

The foyer gradually filled up, young people mostly, some of them looked at me in passing and let their eyes linger longer than they would have if it had been one of their own sitting there. I saw how they turned to mumble to one another afterward, even though they tried to be discreet. Then at last it was so close to the time the film began that there probably wouldn't be anything conspicuous about going in and sitting down. I thought the ticket collector was staring at me as well, but maybe that was something he did with everyone in order to ensure no one tried to sneak by. I was one of the first in the auditorium; there were only the tops of a few people's heads, and a couple or two hanging together like hazelnuts in the semi-darkness. A young man had to stand up so I could get past, he smelled like a gummy bear. When I sat down I could hear the rustle of the packet. The advertisements had already been on for a while and less than half the seats were occupied, and there were quite a number of seats free in the middle, something that made it impossible for me not to think of the lady in the box office: I could picture her behind the bulletproof glass roaring with laughter along with one of her colleagues.

But people continued to pour in, and by the time the last of the lights went out it seemed that the auditorium, which wasn't all that big, was indeed almost full. The film turned out to be a comedy, which is to say that it took a while before I realized that that's what it was, for the simple reason that it wasn't particularly funny at the start. It was as though you had to figure out for yourself that that was what it was supposed to be. But, on the other hand, from then on I was completely under its spell. I thought it was absolutely hilarious, I'd never seen anything like it: the laughter just bubbled up inside me . . . at first I was chuckling . . . then I was gasping for breath . . . more intensely at each new scene . . . finally I was roaring with laughter, whether what they were saying or doing was funny or not. I tried to control myself, but that just made it worse. Now everything was just as uproarious, just as unbearably comic. It was as though I had been possessed by something wholly irresistible, which no longer had anything to do with what was unfolding on the screen . . . save, at most, having been set off by it . . . I was more lying than sitting in my seat. I howled with laughter . . . or gasped silently, because I couldn't catch my breath . . . It was as if the film had cunningly found the key and thrown my door wide open. Finally I had to look away, and in so doing managed to collect myself somewhat. I didn't dare look up, and I tried to avoid listening, for fear of falling victim to a new torrent. Bent over, with my elbows on my knees, and with my eyes fixed on the indeterminable darkness down on the floor between my row and the next, I tried to forget where I was, to turn my thoughts to something else. I dried my tears with my coat sleeve and took great pains to try and direct my thoughts away from anything that might seem funny. I even attempted to think of something really sad I could rally my thoughts around, as a defence against this ruthless devil. A couple of ugly grunts did still escape me, the images from the film flashing like strobes in my memory. But eventually I managed to calm down sufficiently, such that I felt I had overcome the tormentor and would be able to control myself if I made an effort. But still I didn't dare to turn back toward the film again. Even though it had begun to dawn on me that the whole thing was in poor taste and actually quite lowbrow. A bottle rolled by at high speed, the tip of the neck brushed against one of my shoes and changed direction . . . the sound was hollow, like thunder.

I sat up in the chair again, but didn't open my eyes. I heard the voices from the speakers but kept myself from understanding what they said. Now no one in the auditorium was laughing, just as no one had been laughing a little while ago, when I sat bellowing at my worst. Or had they? I couldn't remember. In any event I wouldn't have been able to hear it, the way I'd drowned out the noise of myself and everybody else. Christ, I thought, what must they think of me, all those young couples who had come to enjoy a romantic comedy and had gotten a hysterical lunatic into the bargain, sitting in one of the back rows laughing like he was about to take leave of his senses. I turned my head carefully and opened my eyes slightly, stole a glance at the people to the left of me, and every one of them seemed utterly absorbed with what they were watching . . . they didn't smile once, not one of them, not so much as the faintest ripple at the side of a mouth to be seen . . . they sat there in grave silence and followed the story with youthful attention and empathy.

I squinted cautiously at the screen. And now I couldn't recognise anything, neither the people nor the places, and I wasn't able to pick up the plot from where I'd left off: it was as though a transference, or a transformation, had taken place while I'd been sitting there, bent over, blocking out the world. The only thing I got was that the film was most likely nearing its conclusion. I found that this made me sad, that unmistakeable atmosphere of departure that spread from the screen and down into the auditorium. I heard the rustling of jackets, people already preparing to leave, and that annoyed me: how could they be so sure that this was really the end? . . . that there still wasn't something left? . . . a sudden twist, a little surprise right at the end? But of course they weren't mistaken: immediately after the fade out the first lines of white lettering rose up toward the sky to the accompaniment of cheery music . . . making me feel even more despondent. I thought it was loathsome . . . I didn't want it to end. I wanted a new beginning. Everything over again . . . fresh and unfamiliar . . . without any clues as to how it was going to go . . . what was going to happen . . . no end. Only beginnings. One after the other. That was the way I wanted it. To know that everything was in front of me. That nothing was decided. I didn't want to go . . . I just wanted to stay sitting there, in the dark, and watch film after film after film, without a break, so that the end of one went directly into the beginning of the next. But there was no way back, a queue of people in coats and scarves had already formed beside me, they were standing waiting for the lunatic to get up and go: one of them cleared his throat, conveying their impatience.

At first I was pleasantly surprised when I came out and discovered how early it still was, but this turned to disappointment when I realized how much of the evening was left. I tried to think if there was anyone I could visit, if for no other reason than to kill time. I knew that one of my old friends from school, Bjørn Skogly, lived down around here somewhere, I had his details in my address book, because there'd been talk of arranging some kind of class reunion . . . which fortunately never came about . . . since most of what I can remember from my time at school just makes me feel embarrassed every time I think of it . . . so wouldn't it be fair to expect that it would most likely prove awkward, if I was to call on him now and be invited in for a cup of coffee? Besides, I've always felt slightly disconcerted about visiting people at home, especially for the first time. There's something undignified about it, the way people change as soon as they step over the threshold of their home, how they cast all considerations overboard, relinquish their dignity, put aside everything for which you once liked them, as if they were unhooking the face they show to the world in order to become slack, and obvious, and indifferent. They change their shoes for slippers . . . sit on the sofa with legs akimbo scratching themselves on the stomach . . . belch while they stand in the kitchen to fix a cup of coffee for their guest . . . I'd much rather talk to someone I don't know, I thought, so that all that other stuff is behind me and everything I've said or done earlier doesn't matter anymore. Because then . . . and the mere thought of it warmed me . . . I could, without hesitation, come out and say entirely different things than I would have otherwise . . . I could, quite effortlessly and without a thought for my good name and reputation, come out with statements that had no basis in fact whatsoever, and amuse myself with the reactions I got. I could rattle my sabre and brandish a whip, I thought, and I think I took on a solemn expression as I walked.

I went by the church again, and I saw people on their way up the steps to go inside. I considered going in myself for a moment . . . *perhaps it would change my life*, I thought . . . but I changed my mind when I saw the placard by the entrance announcing that it would be a special service, conducted by a priest from Kenya, followed by music, which you'd expect to be from Kenya as well, although it didn't say anything about that on the placard. I went into a café nearby instead, because I could feel the cold in my bones. I took off my coat and hung it over the back of a chair. Then I sat down, and noticed that this crowded environment put me at ease to a certain degree. I put my hands down on the table beside each other, one was pink and the other, which I'd been holding the bag with, was almost blue in contrast. I ordered a coffee and a packet of cigarettes as well, even though I knew only too well how much you had to fork out for them at places like this . . . but she seemed so considerate, the girl who came over and took my order, that I almost felt obliged to buy something else from her, I thought that a single cup of coffee might be viewed as a slight upon her professional abilities. I studied, not without a certain pleasure, her ample behind as she went back toward the counter . . . the apron enclosing her like a pair of white parentheses . . . while at the same I became aware of a faint smell of urine . . . without looking, I was sure that I had managed to sit down at the table closest to the toilets. But I didn't let it bother me and wasn't under any circumstances about to swap tables, something that was clear to me would seem like the act of a madman, a lonely old fool who couldn't settle down.

The people that had been sitting at the table closest to me were getting ready to leave. They'd eaten quite a large meal, judging by the number of plates on their table. There were two grown women and a boy, or a man rather, who sat in a wheelchair drooling. As one of the women drew him back from the table and turned the wheelchair around a horrible roar emanated from his wet mouth . . . I was very close to answering him, as if his sad howl had provoked a similarly profound and hideous roar from inside myself . . . Both women nodded and smiled to me as they gathered their things to go. They're always so friendly, I thought, the close family of people like that or the ones who look after them. Excessively friendly, as if it's imperative they demonstrate to the world that they've understood something about being a human being that the rest of us, who take sanity for granted, have not. Maybe they think they're more humane . . . by virtue of the burden that's been imposed upon them . . . than the rest of us, who just waltz blithely by? In any case, it's a delight to ask them for their help, for directions somewhere, or if they happen to know what time it is, they seem almost to be filled with an irreducible enthusiasm over being able to help. But *are* they really like that? I couldn't help but wonder . . . whether in reality they've *become* that way because that's the way they want to come across. If they've learned, from their particular experience, that that's the way people should be? Or are they like that because they *have* to be, because their fates dictate it, and their consciences force them, though deep down inside they still have the same contemptible, selfish core as everyone else, it's just that the situation they're in prohibits them from showing it? It was only when the door closed behind the brain-damaged guy and his two caretakers that I realized night had fallen. But when you're with someone like that you're only ever at cafés in the daytime, I thought . . . because it was as though, by way of their considerate retreat, they wanted to leave the place to the ordinary, the carefree, the lonely and confused.

There was a girl sitting on one of the barstools at the counter, with her legs bent under her, like a bird. She kept pushing her hair back behind her ear, as if she really thought that sooner or later it would stay there without falling forward again. She sat listening attentively to another girl, a friend of hers, who was sitting with her back to me. She interrupted now and again to ask a question, when there was something she didn't understand or hadn't quite caught. Then she began to speak, and this allowed me an even better opportunity to study her, to get to know her . . . And despite the fact that I couldn't hear a word she said, I was absolutely certain that I knew how she was expressing herself. It was clear that no matter who she was telling her friend about or what news she was filling her in on . . . and I could see that what she had to say wasn't all good . . . *that she was telling her about them with compassion.* If she was telling her about someone who'd behaved badly or someone who'd made a fool of themselves, then she did so with compassion . . . *with perhaps even greater compassion than if whatever it was hadn't gone wrong.* And she smiled at every opportunity, even emphasized the less cheerful points with a smile . . . she seemed on the whole to be exceptionally understanding, unusually so . . . someone you wouldn't hesitate to confide in, no matter how terrible it might be, the thing that was getting you down. I tried to imagine her name . . . you can just tell with some people, can see that they're a Berit or a Marianne or a Liv . . . but with her, the understanding one, none of the names I thought of seemed to do her justice, even going to extremes like Sunniva or Constance didn't help.

I noticed how uniform and ordinary they all looked, all the other people in the café, when I took my eyes off the girl at the counter and looked around. Hard to tell apart, most of them. Still, I saw the possibility of striking up a conversation with some of them. I thought about things to say. I tried to remember things I'd said to people, the first time I met them. The first time I met Helene for instance, I tried to remember the first thing I'd said to her, the first sentence, or even better, *the very first word.* The woman who had become my wife, what was the very first word she heard me say? If someone had come over and sat down in front of me now, what would be the first thing to pop out of my mouth? If I had to say something in order to avoid an awkward silence what would I resort to then? This thought made me dizzy, the thought of meeting someone, getting to know someone. Her, over by the counter. I thought that if I'd been given the opportunity of falling in love with her, the understanding one, then I could tell her everything about myself from the start, everything over again, while emphasizing the parts that weighed in my favour, and I could have left out those things which, even to this day, I'm ashamed to remember. It would be like a release, I thought, like being set free after a lifetime of captivity. It would be a release from everything that torments you, I thought, everything that usually lies there eating away at your memory. It would be like dying in the world you know and then being reborn in another, where there's nothing written about you yet, where everything is still ahead of you, untouched, unsullied. It's not possible that you're only supposed to have that chance one time in the course of your life, I thought, because then, when you start out, you don't know . . . then you still haven't had the opportunity to understand . . . the possibilities that you're sitting there holding in your hands . . . or should I say that are sitting there on the other side of the table . . . and in any case not when that one time wasn't exactly the real thing, not in the all-consuming way you get the impression that it can be, at its best.

I felt elated and I told myself that from now on anything could happen. Yes, I was so elated that I wouldn't have been surprised if the waitress had come over and said there was a telephone call for me. Oddly enough I had no desire to be drunk. It was as though I made a conscious decision to keep my head clear . . . in case something should happen . . . something that would demand my full attention . . . The understanding one got up to leave. I was disappointed in her. Already? The other one obviously intended to stay, because they said their good-byes inside the café. I still hadn't seen her friend's face, only a lot of dark, wavy hair, and I tried to guess what she looked like, pictured a face not unlike her friend's, a face that went together with the long, dark curls. Just then she turned and starting walking in the direction of the toilets, right toward me, and I nearly fell off my chair, because she was ugly, she was incredibly ugly, her mouth hung half open to reveal enormous gums and she had flushed cheeks too and what looked like a scar running across her whole face, and then a pair of round glasses that magnified her eyes something awful.

I hesitated slightly, but then I ordered another beer. I wondered what you look like, if you sit somewhere for a very long time, alone, just sit, drinking, looking, before, at last, late at night, you take your hat and go, without anything having happened, without having exchanged a single word with anyone. Was it uncommon, or was it maybe something the waitresses and regulars in here saw every single day? Maybe I should go someplace else in a little while, I thought . . . on the other hand I'd much rather stay where I was, seeing as I'd plucked up the courage to come in . . . and now that I'd done that and found an unoccupied table and a comfortable chair, then the best thing I could do was to stay put . . . The smell of urine wasn't so obtrusive anymore either, whether that was because I'd gotten used to it or because it had given way to other, more agreeable odours, I didn't know.

I lit a cigarette . . . I'd forgotten that I'd bought cigarettes . . . and felt a certain relief, at the friendly gestures my own hand made to me at regular intervals. Only to feel even more ill at ease when I put it out and no longer had anything to do. I noticed I was beginning to feel hot, so hot that I began to sweat . . . a drop slid out of my armpit and scurried downward like a frightened little insect . . . and, as if that in itself had been the decisive thing, I now felt entirely demoralized . . . my entrance into this vile establishment was starting to look like the biggest mistake of the day, so far . . . and it seemed all that was left of my previous elation were some pathetic embers.

I've actually always been waiting for an accident, I thought, and have almost taken it for granted that sooner or later something terrible would happen that would leave us completely crushed. As though I've been living in fear of it and wishing for it at the same time. In any case, it's something I've been thinking about almost incessantly since we started a family and as a consequence had reason to worry. The absence of this tragedy has, thus far, only strengthened my belief in it. When Marit and Nina were small I was just walking around waiting for it to happen, because everything was going so smoothly . . . they were hardly ever sick, and both of them did well at school . . . no one had any dramatic experiences . . . never any serious injuries . . . never any disappearances or near accidents . . . never any trouble at school . . . never any drugs, never anything that caused the police, God forbid, to enter into the picture. I waited, and watched, and thought: the reason it's going so well with them is only because fate is sitting there saving up for an enormous tragedy. Good fortune is only shining on us in order to maximise the contrast, so that the transition to hell will be as abrupt, and as brutal, and as shocking as possible. I waited, and nothing happened. I waited, and for every year that passed without major incident, it was as though I could feel the weight of yet another load being placed on the beam, which, one fine day, would break our back. Is it a remnant from childhood . . . it must be, where else could it come from? . . . this belief that one day I'd pay dearly for all the things I've somehow avoided being exposed to?

I tried to remember what they looked like, my daughters. But, try as I might, I couldn't manage, it was as if neither of them could be coaxed out. I tried to picture Helene's face . . . I figured that if I started there, with her familiar features, then it couldn't possibly be all that far to Marit and Nina, because isn't that how it is, don't daughters bear a closer resemblance to their mothers than to their fathers? But now I couldn't even manage to picture her . . . I tried with all my might, and it felt as if I was ever so close to her but still couldn't get around that last corner . . . like some spiteful dream . . . A mishmash of everything, a shapeless face in which I still thought I could recognise something, but could never say to myself with certainty that that's her . . . *that's them . . . this is them . . . this is what they look like, my two children* . . . who both stopped being children a long time ago of course, yes, and who perhaps at this very moment were standing in front of a mirror examining their first wrinkles for all I knew, they've always been vain, both of them. Yes, it became a shapeless, grotesque face that seemed to mock the sincerity of my endeavour.

I tried to think of any incidents from their childhood, any funny or poignant episodes: the sorts of thing you went around telling other people when you wanted to put your children in a good light, little examples of how advanced they were for their age, how quickly they picked things up, which special talents lay in their little hands waiting to blossom. But I couldn't think of anything . . . No, I had to admit to myself that I couldn't manage to recall a single notable episode . . . I wasn't able to pull any charming antics or indeed a single act of mischief out of my hat. The more I tried to think of something and came up with nothing the more unwell I felt. I tried to think of some of the arrangements Helene and I had made about practical matters . . . the division of responsibilities, who was going to do what at which times, those sorts of thing . . . as a way of getting closer, indirectly, to what had gone on. But no, I couldn't even remember if a babysitter had ever set foot in our house. How is it possible, I thought, to forget so much of what must have taken up most of our time and attention for so long? Because it must have done, with two prima donnas like that, and with them being so close in age. Or had it? I tried to think if perhaps we had sent them away for any length of time . . . as a possible explanation for the gaping holes in my memory . . . but I couldn't remember anything like that either and besides it wouldn't be nearly enough to explain my failing memory, because the truth was . . . and the admission made me squirm . . . that this wasn't about some *holes in my memory*, but a single gaping chasm of oblivion from which nothing, at least not at this moment, had the power to claw its way up over the edge and into the light of consciousness.

I went to the men's room . . . it wasn't far to walk . . . and splashed some cold water on my face. I found I needed to nip into a stall as well. Once I was in there I stood staring right at the white tiles, glistening as if they'd been covered in oil. I imagined the harsh urine-scented light was shining right through me, as though forcing me to be aware of the bones in my arm, through the flesh packed around them. All the way out to my fingertips, which gripped my organ while I sprayed myself empty . . . bones that grew thinner and thinner until finally they were just points at the ends, right under my nails . . . under the hand, pulled on like a glove. I could see them clearly . . . and knew that it was true . . . that it was a skeleton standing there, leaning against the wall in one of the bathroom stalls. In order to drive this vision away . . . or was that really the reason? . . . I did something I hadn't done in . . . God knows how long . . . after first, of course, having made sure the door was securely locked . . . It wouldn't exactly have calmed me down if the door was flung open and I'd been caught red-handed. I thought about the waitress at the first café, and then about the waitress at this place . . . finally both of them . . . and it didn't take long. I stood there quite soberly and looked at my own discharge, my trousers very nearly on again before I was entirely finished. I avoided looking in the mirror on the way out.

If it wasn't quite like the place had changed totally, then it was like hours had passed since I'd gone to the toilet. Now the café was almost completely full; loud music was playing, but the noise of everyone sitting talking and shouting to each other was even louder; smoke hung over their heads, it was dark outside, and the windows were black. But maybe it was only because I'd in- stinctively held onto the impression I'd gotten of the place when I arrived there earlier in the evening, when it was still sparsely occupied and the room had a lot of daylight and activity outside it; maybe I'd been sitting trying to hold on to that atmosphere without noticing that it had gradually changed. Now it seemed darkness had fallen and that night-time indulgences were already underway. I was also surprised to discover that my table had been taken, two girls . . . with mouths like bleeding wounds . . . who obviously hadn't seen, or had chosen to ignore, the coat lying in plain sight on the chair opposite. At first I considered taking my coat and leaving . . . and thereafter I considered sitting down and politely pointing out that the table was occupied . . . but in the end I just sat down, and nodded to them both, by way of a greeting, which probably seemed self-conscious and slightly clumsy. They looked at each other and giggled . . . the wounds opened . . . and then immediately one of them wanted to know what my name was. Her directness caught me off guard and I answered, asking them their names in turn. They told me their names, but judging by the laughter and the furtive glances they exchanged, they seemed to have made them up right there and then. All the giggling annoyed me, they were bubbling over constantly, and I got it into my head that it was me they were laughing at . . . which was probably true . . . and that they already saw me as an inexhaustible source of entertainment. I had to admit, with regret, that they were uncouth, the kind who are only interested in finding things to laugh at and who laugh all the louder the simpler their jokes. At the same time I couldn't avoid being affected by their vivacity, because there was something lively and high-spirited about their impertinence . . . nor could I help feeling a trifle flattered by the attention, even though it primarily consisted of their seeing me as highly unusual . . . they must have thought I was a real oddball, or just out of place, here in their hangout, yes, at their *usual table* for all I knew . . . maybe that was why they were laughing? We sat like that for a while exchanging a few words on subjects that were so insignificant and undefined that I'd already forgotten them the moment we moved onto the next thing. And when the waiter elbowed his way through to us . . . a man this time, which annoyed me . . . I was generous enough to order yet another glass of beer, as well as a coffee, because now more than ever I was determined to keep a cool head.

They wanted to talk about animation, they were obviously very interested in animated films, and it seemed as though they wanted me to join in the conversation. But now I really thought they were stupid, both of them. I saw how young they were, *young at heart* in a sense, because I presumed they were closer to thirty than twenty, and I thought: how childish and ignorant . . . how *foolish* can you possibly allow yourself to be when you're at an age when most people have long since started a family and are bound hand and foot? Then things took a turn, and I perceived them in exactly the opposite way, that on the contrary they were quite bright, and I felt indescribably stupid sitting there trying to take part in an intelligent conversation about animated films. Moreover, I soon learned that animated films didn't just mean cartoons any longer. After a while I became quite impressed with how they held forth on this subject, a subject I . . . due to ignorance, I now understood . . . hadn't expected could prompt anything more than a few fairly banal observations. Whereas with these two there was no stopping them once they'd started. A multitude of names I'd never heard before whizzed over my head. I readily allowed myself be entertained, asked a few questions now and again, and declared my lack of knowledge with a motion of my hand every time they tried to question me more closely about my opinion. I saw then that I was about to actually engage with their conversation, whether because they so insisted on involving me, or because I for my own part had really begun to get interested, to such a degree that we might just remain sitting together for a while longer and constitute a group, *a table* . . . the three of us. And I suddenly remembered that it hadn't been more than an hour since I had in fact been sitting in the darkness of a cinema: I was about to tell them this but thought better of it . . . I thought I could already hear how foolish the story would sound if I tried to put it into words . . . and once again that word, *cinema*, filled me with horror, without my being able to grasp what was behind it . . .

When we'd finished our drinks the girls wanted to order another round, and this time I offered to buy, I didn't want any more myself, for the time being, but I said that they could have what they wanted and I'd pay. They ordered beer, and I asked if they were sure they didn't want anything else as well, and then one of them ordered a whisky, and the other . . . whom I'd begun to regard as the more likeable of the two . . . a liqueur. They smiled now, both of them, and laughed at everything that was said, and that made me happy, and there was no problem, I had enough money. The fact that they wanted to drink was reassuring, the way I looked at it was that at least it meant they wouldn't become less candid or lively as the night went on. They asked me what my name was again. I noticed that the more likeable of the two began to take over more and more, that increasingly it was her who addressed me, that all in all she seemed more eager to include me than the other one. At the same time I noticed how adroit she was in making sure she had her friend's attention, every time she turned to me, as if she was engaged in a kind of game that was intended for her, and that this was what they were laughing at all the time, her mock flirt with me, and I couldn't escape the thought that the amusing thing about the situation, as far as they were concerned, was that under normal circumstances it would have been *simply inconceivable* for her to flirt with someone like me. But I was never quite sure what it was, the signals she sent me were too veiled and ambiguous for that, and the whole time I felt myself alternating between feeling honoured and feeling duped. They asked me my name three more times. I said something, which I myself thought was stupid, but they didn't laugh at it. Then I tried to think of something shocking to tell them, because to me they seemed like the sort who'd be impressed by the grotesque. I remember telling Elise and Hans-Jacob something once, and that I'd soon got carried away and started to exaggerate, I mean really exaggerate, because just for once I wanted to outdo the story of Kristoffer, I hadn't held back on any of the grisly details, while at the same time, and not without a certain degree of satisfaction, I sat studying Elise, who I recall, just grew paler and paler. But I couldn't remember this story, and anyway it was unlikely to make the same impression on my two young friends, the worldly party animals that they were. As an experiment, however, I don't know, or perhaps by way of a replacement . . . I regretted it immediately in any case . . . I told them about Kristoffer and the accident . . . and I exaggerated that too, because now I thought that it wouldn't meet with their expectations if they were after something truly horrific. It was a cheap trick, I was aware of that, and if it made more of an impression on them for it I don't know . . . they listened politely while I told them the details, but it didn't have any effect on their mood as far as I could see. Then they started whispering to one another, and this, I noticed, irritated me so much that I felt I might really lose my temper if they continued. The thought that I'd stood them a round fanned the flames of my resentment. But then she turned to me again, the likeable one . . . took my hand even . . . looked me in the eyes and smiled, didn't laugh, far as I could see . . . a distinction that had acquired tremendous importance for me over the last hour . . . and then she said that she was glad that we'd met, and that so far tonight had been a special night.

I was almost ashamed over how little it took to placate me. In any case, all my scepticism about the likeable one and her ambiguous advances now vanished entirely. I was, in short . . . for a little while anyway . . . wholly *hers*. All the giggling and whispering and all the silliness was forgotten. All the inappropriate looks they'd exchanged were forgotten. I bought another round of drinks, though again abstaining myself. The likeable one wanted a different liqueur, the other one another whisky. The girls complained . . . why wouldn't I drink together with them? I found myself thinking that the whisky would most probably make the other one very drunk, while hopefully the liqueur would keep the likeable one at just the right level of tipsy for the rest of the night. The difference between them, it seemed to me, just grew. Now it was as though there were at least ten years between them. Where the likeable one was calm, the other one was restless and wound-up. Where the likeable one was enthusiastic, the other one was sluggish and passive, and always seemed to get insecure, I noticed, when her friend was at her most animated, whether her excitement was phony or sincere. This insecurity wasn't so much down to envy or jealousy, I thought . . . as it was to a feeling of being let down. It was as though she, the likeable one, had let her, the other one, down with her newfound gravitas, and that the intimacy and trust that to start off with had clearly defined the line between them, from the same world, and me, the outsider, I nearly said *enemy*. Maybe this was reinforced by the fact that the other one was now beginning to feel left out, she certainly couldn't have helped but notice that more and more of the conversation was taking place between me and the likeable one, on her initiative mind you, I let her take the lead, for fear that anything I might have come up with would bore her and thus sever the rapport between us, because after all I wasn't so dazzled that I couldn't see that it was hanging by a thread.

I glanced at her, the other one, surreptitiously, and it was plain to see that she was now so drunk she'd reached the point where the kind of mood you're in is critical, because from there on in it would only be amplified further, for the better or for the worst, ever-increasing exaltation or the opposite, a darker and darker melancholy. And it wasn't hard to see where she was headed that night. Her head had already started to hang and her eyes were fixed on the coaster that her glass had rested upon, and which she was turning slowly, slowly around with her fingers. The sight of her gave me a loathsome sense of satisfaction, like a tingle down in the pit of my stomach. The dosage had had the expected effect. The likeable one seemed to have almost forgotten her. There was no trace left of the giggling intimacy. I couldn't help seeing the words *good investment*, they flashed like an advertising sign above her head. And suddenly she stood up, the other one, bumping into the table so hard she almost knocked the glasses over, stared at me with glassy eyes, and disappeared out of the café, stiff as a board.

The likeable one didn't dignify the scene with more than a fairly indifferent shrug of the shoulders, something I interpreted as being entirely in my favour. She didn't seem to regret it in any case, nor to give any thought to going after her. It felt like a victory. I'd managed to pull off, somehow, almost imperceptibly, the discreet little trick of wrenching her loose from her best friend, whom she obviously was usually almost stuck to, in that crudest of ways, in the way only grown women who are childish for their age can be. It was a delight to see . . . because there was no mistaking it . . . how her self-respect grew, the likeable one's, as soon as she was released from the weight of her friend, who otherwise curbed her dignity and prevented it from finding expression. It was as though she'd straightened up, right there in her chair, it was as though she'd matured right in front of my eyes, discarded all that girlish nonsense and took on a serious expression about her lips, which had been a crimson red . . . that was the first thing I'd noticed when I came out of the bathroom . . . of which now only a dry, pink scab remained. She wasn't particularly pretty, I could see that now . . . but it seemed the absence of that characteristic, which otherwise would almost certainly have dominated my impression of her, only made it easier to relate to her, since I could now concentrate all my attention on listening, understanding, answering, on being on a par. It's true, I was really striving, based on my own simplistic understanding of such things, to be *on a par.*

I looked around. I wondered what they thought, people who saw us, me and her, left alone, preoccupied, as we probably seemed to them, with one another. But nobody paid us any mind, nobody so much as glanced at us in passing, as far as I could tell . . . everyone was preoccupied themselves. I was sitting, I noticed, with my hands folded on the tabletop, with my coffee cup well sheltered in the triangular harbour my arms had formed. Mildly embarrassed by my discovery, I loosened my grip and took a sip of the coffee, which was stone cold. Now I could feel time slipping through my fingers. I was terrified of boring her, of her suddenly seeing me for what I was and losing interest in me. I was terrified that that young and adult mouth, which had nearly bled out, would open to form its first, irresistible, tell-tale yawn and with that pass a death sentence on an evening which had brought so many surprises so far, most of them positive. At the same time I noticed that I was expecting something of her . . . that since this evening, so full of surprises, had already taken us so far, then it was probably because something was going to happen between us . . . and I wasn't necessarily thinking of anything erotic . . . that thought hadn't entered my mind . . . but all the same, I felt I was sitting there nursing an expectation of some sort concerning our meeting . . . the expectation of a return on my investment . . . in the evening, in her, in my departure from all common practice, in fate, which had ushered us into meeting, yes, exactly, *a dividend*, of some kind or other . . . a lengthy, deep conversation perhaps, which would alter my perception of certain subjects on some essential points.

I didn't feel that I could just leave everything up to her anymore, that it was probably just as much up to me to bring up some really interesting point, now that we'd been left alone and she didn't have the other one there to back her . . . If the conversation came to a halt, yes, if there was so much as a pause that lasted a little too long, I was afraid we'd discover that we no longer had anything to talk about. But it bothered me too, the fact that I'd begun thinking so carefully about the situation we were in, I saw it as a sign of weakness, it made it seem as though the . . . situation . . . had now inevitably lost some of that freshness which earlier in the evening had drowned out all other impressions. The impulsive and frivolous atmosphere around her . . . *around us* . . . had to be regained at all costs. Above all I would have liked to have seen her sitting the way she had been the first time I caught sight of her, vulgar and nonchalant, with those pouting red lips, giggling at the gravity of life. The image of those two coquettes sitting there when I came back from the bathroom . . . *as if they were waiting for me* . . . filled me with a sort of sweet melancholy, as if I was about to come to the realization that the evening was already over, that I'd already gotten whatever I was entitled to, that there wasn't any hope of anything more. *Giggling at the gravity of life* . . . I turned it over in my mind. Was that what I had always felt the urge to do, but had never quite managed? To laugh in the face of fate? To respond to its deadly seriousness with a chuckle that was carefree enough to eclipse it? I had a vague suspicion that I'd never dared to do anything other than take it to heart, whatever happened me, the cheerful as well as the cheerless. And it seemed to me I'd never experienced anything that, sooner or later, hadn't made me sad. Even in my happiest moments I'd been sad. When things had worked out as well as they could, I'd still feel dejected and disheartened, because this never came about without interminable planning and toil, without exhaustive and painstaking preparation of things that, if I thought about it, should actually have fallen into place by themselves.

I thought of Marit, and of what I had said to her when we'd met. Had she told Karl-Martin? Were they going around still waiting to hear word? Had she called Nina and told her, discussed whether or not they should believe it? What had Nina said? Had she brushed it aside, told Marit not to waste her time thinking about it, that it was probably just talk, nothing serious? That is, if they still kept in touch, still met up from time to time, her and Nina. Nina, who . . . I had to admit . . . has, after all, always been a sort of favourite. Come to think of it, I've never actually been particularly fond of Marit . . . her intrigues and tricks were too crude for that, her duplicity too easy to see through, and her ambition so relentless that it wasn't difficult to see something like brutality in it, the times you caught a glimpse. With Nina . . . with her it was different . . . at least with her I'd shared some moments where we had, if not complete and utter trust, then at least had some form of respect for each other, a kind of equality, if you could call it that. I thought about going to see her . . . maybe even tonight . . . why not? . . . I could call Marit and get her address, if she had it . . . yes . . . leave the café and try to track her down . . . it was now or never, I felt, as I considered it. Where was she . . . Nina . . . right at this moment? Was she in bed at her own place, together with a man? Was she travelling and spending the night among strangers? Or maybe she was out on the town like her father, sitting drinking wine someplace here in town, not far from the likeable one and me? I have to find her, I thought. I have to find her and talk to her. We've never gotten to talk properly together. We never really got started. I tried to picture her, free and easy and full of life in the company of friends, in a smoke-filled café like this one . . . but how was I supposed to picture her . . . without it turning grotesque . . . since her last few years at home she hadn't shown me anything other than an ice-cold face expressing no emotion save a desire to control, her vehement demand to have things exactly the way she wanted. That was the last thing I'd seen, that stony face. While at the moment . . . perhaps . . . she was sitting somewhere in the world, smiling and laughing with all of her heart. Or was she? I had to speak to her, I felt, not just about that, but about everything. So many years had passed since those last confrontations at home, there couldn't be anything standing in the way of our setting aside our pride . . . both of us! . . . and starting from scratch, abandoning our positions and seeing eye to eye, talking openly like adults, not as a father and daughter who must continue to deceive one another. And I found myself taking a look around the café, in the vain hope of catching sight of her at one of the tables.

She leaned over toward me now, the likeable one, pulled at my sleeve like a spoiled child, wanted more to drink, obviously, even though she didn't say it in so many words. I signalled to the waiter, hoping to myself that it would take a little time before she . . . no . . . he came. It seemed as though she'd soon have had enough too, the likeable one. She kept pulling at my arm, even though she must have seen that I'd already signalled. And she started talking at me again, saying that I had to drink as well, not just sit there like some wet blanket from the west coast, or whatever idiotic expression she used. When the waiter finally came, she asked for two liqueurs for herself. It'll take him such a long time to come back again anyway, she explained after he'd left. While I . . . and it wasn't because I felt like it, but more out of a secret desire to be demonstrative in one way or another, to tease her a bit, put her in her place, I'm not quite sure . . . asked for a glass of water with ice for myself, just that, nothing else. She looked at me as if offended . . . accused me, wordlessly, of having ruined the evening. And maybe that was exactly what I felt like doing . . . ruining the evening, nothing less. She drank the liqueur as if it was aquavit . . . *threw it back*. At the same time I couldn't quite understand why she should express such disappointment that I'd controlled myself, limited my alcohol intake and . . . maybe . . . showed the first signs of wanting to bring things to an end, of maybe splitting up and leaving in not so long. Was she . . . also . . . about to get so drunk that she no longer had any idea where she was, who she was with, and why she was sitting here? When I thought about it I had no clue how much a girl of that age can drink . . . maybe I should've known better and cut off the supply long ago? Then it hit me that it was possible that . . . since she had stayed . . . after her friend had gone home . . . or at least I hoped that's what she'd done! . . . then it was important to her as well that something happened between us, so that she'd have something to tell her friend, preferably something sensational . . . something worth bragging a little bit about at least . . . to her friend who just hadn't lived up to expectations this evening, and as a consequence, had missed out on the whole adventure. I could imagine it was important for her, the likeable one, not to return home empty-handed . . . that the next day she could leave her friend in no doubt as to whether it had proved worthwhile staying behind with the mysterious stranger . . . or would she say: *that bashful wet blanket?* Or would she remember my name and use it? I could well imagine that one of the alternatives, as she saw it, to having a real experience was at least to make certain of having as many drinks bought for her as she could manage to consume in the course of the evening, that in itself would be a good enough story, I suppose, because something like that couldn't possibly be an everyday occurrence . . . not in this day and age . . . even for coquettes of their kind. Perhaps, if she'd set her sights high enough, she was hoping for something erotic to occur after all, though I had a hard time picturing that possibility . . . and neither had she made any passes at me, even when she was at her most vulgar. There must be something, I thought, and told myself it was quite clear that other motives lay behind her feline behaviour, that she wanted more than the mere entertainment of our being together.

My heart sank when I saw what time it was . . . why? . . . I had the whole night ahead of me, if I wanted. I checked the inside pocket of my coat. Then I looked at the faces around the nearby tables, one after another, as if once again I hoped to see Nina there. And why not, I thought. Would that actually have been so strange, that we had . . . by chance . . . ended up in the same café this evening . . . found each other again, here, after so many years? No more surprising than going an entire year *without* meeting someone you know who lives in the same city, whether it was on the street or someplace else. Taking encouragement from this simple fact, I took a good look around . . . but had, of course, to give up again. I took comfort in the fact that it was probably for the best . . . because there was no telling what she'd think of her father after being out of touch with him for several years, if she had met me here now, tonight. Or, I thought, would she be so surprised and so happy about finding me here, in a situation like this . . . she'd probably have drawn her own conclusions and given the likeable one a sideways glance . . . that this would be just what was needed in order to break the ice between us . . . clear away our strained past and bring us together again?

The likeable one kept on nagging, but in such an incoherent way that I didn't understand what she said, it was like she was chewing more than speaking. She was on the verge of beginning to irritate me, something I hoped she'd soon realize. But she was well on her way to being exactly like her friend. All of a sudden the whole thing seemed a bit meaningless to me, that I'd supplied two young girls with alcohol for an entire evening, only to see . . . first one . . . then the other . . . stumble out the door like the living dead. But it didn't matter, I didn't have anything else to spend the money on anyway. And no one could tell me that it hadn't been a memorable night, at times, invigorating.

Because of that thought about money, I contemplated then, for the first time in my life . . . I think . . . inheritance. Even if we didn't leave much behind us, then there'd probably still be enough for Nina and Marit to fight over, if they wanted to, if nothing unforeseen happened. Or should I have an ingenious will drawn up, something really cunning, built upon a series of eccentric conditions, enough to have both my daughters tearing out their hair when the time came . . . by way of returning the compliment, the last word after all their unanswered insolence? The thought amused me. Maybe I'd give everything to somebody else, bequeath every penny to an institution or a good cause in order to really put one over on them, just leave them a little something each, something completely worthless, as a final joke. I could picture them in the lawyer's office, dressed up for the occasion, with their two greedy husbands sitting in their cars outside waiting, both women turning green in the face because of what they're hearing, and which the lawyer has to repeat several times in order to convince them, that yes, that's what's written here. Why shouldn't I? When you've lived an entire life, as dutifully as you could, in accordance with all the rules and regulations, shouldn't you then be allowed to indulge in a little malice as you bring the whole thing to a close, a coarse jest, if for no other reason than to stand out a little, when it's all over in any case? Wouldn't it all have been pretty much a waste of time otherwise, all that good behaviour, if you died just as respectable as you'd lived? It's so easy to hold onto your childhood faith that some reward is coming, I thought. It's so easy to believe that happiness and propriety go hand in hand. That if you live your life as a good person, then you'll get a good life in return, like a prize . . .

The woman facing me waved her empty glass around . . . the second one, she'd drunk up both . . . and gave me her most radiant smile. And I couldn't help but let myself be readily deceived. But before I ordered again, I placed my hand on her shoulder, put on my most authoritative and paternal voice, and asked her if she didn't think she'd already had enough. I didn't catch her answer, but it was probably pretty rude, judging by the look she gave me. I leaned back reluctantly and ordered, of course, another round . . . and a liqueur for myself . . . she brightened up when she heard that. I figured that this was the last round anyhow, that after that it'd be time to say a polite thank you for a nice time, take my coat and my bag, and leave.

Suddenly she started asking me all kinds of questions . . . about what I did, if I was married, where I lived, if I had children . . . the sort of things that are everyone's business, and which . . . for that reason? . . . I don't know . . . I found disappointing, I mean that she'd start bothering with them only now. She even asked me how old I was, as if she wanted to know the story of my life. Why? We'd been sitting there all night, first the three of us, and now the two of us, without talking about that kind of thing, and it dawned on me that that's what I had liked so much, how impersonal the whole thing had been. That we were able, without any fuss, to talk together even though we didn't know each other. But at the same time I felt I could retrieve it if it proved necessary, the good humour I'd been in earlier in the evening . . . maybe because of the liqueur, maybe because the likeable one was now involved in our conversation again in earnest, and not just talking nonsense. She didn't get that much out of me, but we kept it going until we'd finished our drinks. Then she stood up . . . and I expected . . . hoped? . . . that she would make much the same exit as her friend. But instead she leaned over me . . . *did she want to kiss me?* . . . and rested her elbow on my shoulder . . . *the way a whore leans into a car* . . . but only said "excuse me for a second" and disappeared into the ladies' room. I sat there at a loss for a while. I looked at my watch a number of times. Finally she'd been in there so long that I figured that this was my opportunity to slip out unnoticed and leave her, while at the same time I had to be prepared, since so much time had passed, for her to appear at any second through the door right across from me. I fumbled for my bag under the table and put it on my lap. I counted to ten. Then I put one arm through the sleeve of my coat, the one farthest from the door, and remained sitting like that, ready to pull it out again if the door opened. I moved my bag from one hand to the other, and slowly, slowly wriggled my other arm down into the other sleeve. Now I only needed to give my shoulders a quick shrug, and I'd have my coat on. I did that while at the same time I pushed my chair back from the table with my feet. I patted my chest once more in order to check if the wad of notes was there. Then I stood up and started walking in the direction of the exit, I'd mapped out the path I wanted to take . . . and banged my knee against the corner of a table because it was so narrow there . . . but I clenched my teeth . . . and then I was outside. I enjoyed the feeling of the cold air, it tasted like toothpaste in my mouth. From where I stood I could see right into the café, the yellow room where I'd been sitting so long it was as though I hadn't been anywhere else in weeks, the image etched into my brain. And I saw the likeable one come out of the door in there and go and sit down at our table. As far as I could see she didn't seem surprised that I wasn't there, it didn't appear that she was looking around for me anyway. The only explanation could be that she'd thought I'd gone to take a leak as well, and that she was sitting waiting for me to come back. I felt sorry for her, and stood there for a while looking at her, she was sitting with her back to me. Now she turned, half toward the window, so that I could see her face. A familiar face, I thought, it too was etched into my brain. She was a beautiful woman, that was plain to see, but I didn't like her, I was aware of that now.

There was a row of taxis in the square, their bright signs were tempting but it was completely out of the question. I could waste money on the young girls all right, but not on a taxi with the fare starting at thirty kroners, or whatever their evening and night-time rates were nowadays . . . not as long as I was fit enough to walk. It was cold, it grew colder for every block I put behind me, as if months were passing as I walked, and I was approaching the winter that lay in wait at the end of the streets. I passed a few people, but not many. The first newspapers were already lying in a bundle in front of a newsstand that wouldn't be opening for hours yet. VANISHED ran the headline in white letters on a black background . . . the girl's eyes just about visible above the fold. I couldn't help myself, I turned the bundle over in order to see the rest: WITHOUT TRACE . . . and saw her nose and a mouth . . . a neck with the collar of a white blouse around it. But it was the last two words that made the biggest impression on me, I thought about it the whole way home.

I decided to take the stairs, probably for no other reason than a completely natural anxiety about taking the lift alone at night-time . . . you just take it for granted that there's a bigger chance of its breaking down then, don't you? The newspaper lay there, bulging, at an angle across the doormat, I bent down and put it under my arm, and even though I was out of breath, I couldn't help but feel a certain satisfaction at the thought of the distance I'd covered on foot . . . it was a good few kilometres . . . even though when you're in the city you've a hard time imagining that anywhere is far away.

The first thing I did was kick my shoes off. My feet, I noticed, were cold and sweaty, so I took my socks off too, rolled them up and shoved them in under the chest of drawers in front of the mirror. I spread out my toes, which felt like they were made of wax. I stood there for a while, finding just the right point over my feet where the odour was strongest, and sniffed, not without a certain pleasure, because even though it was disgusting, it was also pleasant, albeit in a pervasive way, reminiscent of . . . prunes . . . prune compote. When I opened my eyes again, I caught sight of the smoke detector peeking carefully down from one of the rafters. I took the chair out from under the jackets and coats, clambered up onto it, and pressed the bright red button . . . not so much to check the batteries as to as to allow myself the childish thrill of the brief electronic peep. Then I walked down the hall . . . making sure to be extra quiet when passing the bedroom door . . . and into the kitchen, where I tossed the newspaper, in an almost audacious sort of way, so it landed with a thud on the kitchen counter, before I turned the lights on . . . safe in the knowledge that there were two rooms between me and where my wife lay . . . hopefully . . . fast asleep. But now that I was standing there, having come safely past, I felt a sudden pang of disappointment that she was sleeping so soundly . . . *that she was sleeping* at all, and wasn't sitting up waiting for me, beside herself with worry, such intense worry that it would turn to anger as soon as she set eyes on me. Had she really not been afraid of what could have happened? Had she not even gotten in touch with anyone? Asked if I was there, or reported me missing?

The coffeemaker was filled with water, and the kitchen table was set for two. In other words everything was as it should be . . . at least for her . . . I pushed one of the plates out of the way to make space for my arms. My ears were ringing, I noticed that now, since I couldn't hear a thing, not a sound, no clattering of cups, no rumbling from the vacuum cleaner, no radio on, no cascades of laughter from the TV, no revving of car engines from the courtyard below, not even any muffled sounds from the other apartments. The only thing that, after a long while, broke the almost scary silence was the distant howl of a train . . . in a flash I saw the yellow windows rush past, with people asleep in contorted positions. I opened the fridge without leaving my seat, pulled out a carton of milk, and took a few swigs. I saw a white bowl with clingfilm over it on the bottom shelf, and I noticed that

I was hungry, but I couldn't be bothered . . . couldn't be bothered to get up . . . couldn't be bothered to take food out . . . couldn't be bothered to eat . . . I pulled my shirt collar right up to my nose . . . what on earth would I say to Helene? I didn't want to think about it, I'd probably be able to come up with some story or another, if sufficient pressure was brought to bear. I wasn't tired, on the contrary I felt wide awake. But at the same time I was too tired to do anything . . . do anything? . . . do what exactly, right now, in the middle of the night? So I just sat like that, for a long time, studying the room closely, the way I imagined an investigator would, if there'd been a crime committed here. I let my eyes wander slowly over everything there . . . Helene's Post-it notes hanging all over . . . she tended to those notes like a garden . . . weeding out and planting anew . . . the rubber towel holders, the spice rack, the brown knife block, the plates and glasses stacked in the sink, the kitchen clock with its florid numbers, the radio on the shelf above the paper-towel roll, a green plant in the laundry sink that was far too cramped for its long leaves . . . are they still called leaves when they get that long? . . . she'd probably put it there in order to water it. Then I got the feeling that there really *was* something criminal about what I was doing. There was something unseemly about sitting there, with the light on, in the middle of the night, like I was disturbing something that was usually left in peace, protected by darkness and silence. It was as though all this . . . all these things . . . lived secret lives at night that no one was meant to see. At the same time there was something wonderful, yes, wonderful about sitting there alone, completely alone at last . . . knowing that nobody could disturb the peace and quiet . . . it was as though I was hearing music . . . music that was made especially for me and which would never be played again . . .

I thought of the likeable one and I felt a sort of sadness . . . as if I'd lost her. She had after all kept me company for an entire evening, yet it was highly unlikely we'd ever see each other again. But at the same time I had to admit I wasn't altogether sure if I would have wanted to meet her again, if I was given the opportunity. Her hands, I recalled, had looked old, her knuckles clearly visible, the skin dry, as if covered in scales . . . it had crossed my mind, although I dismissed the thought, that they could be the hands of an *old woman*. I pictured her in a room, together with her friend, curled up together in bed while the likeable one related what had happened. I took it for granted that she'd alter a lot, that she'd leave out some things and exaggerate others, and I wondered what it would end up sounding like, our evening, in her version. I was embarrassed to think of how long I'd been with her . . . it wasn't something you did, sit like that all evening, without it taking on a particular significance . . . so openly as well, as if we were carrying on and showing it off to the whole world.

I stood up and stretched my legs, my feet made a sticky sound as they came free of the floor. It still bothered me, the idea that something decisive needed to happen before the night was at an end . . . it felt necessary, if I was to see any meaning in what I'd been through. I went over to the cooker. A stain on the white enamel had crept into my field of vision. I bent over to take a look at it, and I saw that it resembled a demon . . . a little, mocking demon . . . crouching down and waving at me. I stood for a while looking at him. He stared back defiantly. Then I got the dishcloth from the sink and scrubbed him off . . . rubbing for a long time before I'd gotten it all. The dishcloth smelled sour and the smell lingered on my fingers afterward. I looked at the clock, at the coffeemaker and at the fridge. And back again the same way . . . fridge . . . coffeemaker . . . clock . . . It'd be so easy to leave Helene now, I thought. Just as easy as it was to say it to Marit that day, without a thought for the consequences. Maybe there was some meaning behind the way I'd just blurted it out. I could get it done in an hour, make sure I took only the most important things with me, maybe write a note and hang it up on the fridge door, among the coppice of her own epistles . . . and then sneak out, just as carefully as I'd come in . . . All this . . . *the great leap* . . . in complete silence, while she slept so soundly in there, making that distinctive whistling noise through her nose that can still frighten the life out of me at night . . . it sounds like a woman screaming a few rooms away.

Tiredness came over me. In the old days, I thought, I always looked forward to it getting so late that I could justify going to bed, so that my conscience would allow me to let fatigue get the better of me: it couldn't be *too* early, though, or else you'd just start to feel old. I used to loan Helene my sweater at night . . . she was always so cold . . . it was still warm from my body when she put it on after we'd gotten ready for bed . . . it went down to her knees, like a little dress . . . before she ran across the cold floor, jumped into bed, and hid under the duvet. It was strange, almost unpleasant, I remember, lying like that in semi-darkness and being aware of my own smell coming from her.

The thought of getting up, getting ready, and getting on the tram in just a few hours, filled me with horror, I really wasn't sure if I could manage it. If only it was still the weekend. I was put in mind of our Sundays, when Helene always gets up before me . . . the first thing I do as soon as I feel the mattress rock as she gets ready to get up is to turn over, without actually being awake, so that I can stretch out at an angle over the whole bed. I don't know why, but there's a particular enjoyment to be had in lying diagonally across the bed . . . maybe it's the knowledge that you're finally taking possession of the whole thing, after having been so considerate in keeping to your own side all night long? I lie there, more anesthetized than asleep, until I hear the door open and the smell of coffee begins to waft in . . . Then I turn over onto my back, kick the duvet off and lie there a little longer . . . until I almost feel cold . . . which is the last thing I need to hurry me up out of bed, put on my dressing gown and slippers, and go out, to the kitchen, where everything is laid out on the table.

I glanced up at the clock. Five minutes more and another hour would have passed. The ticking was infernal. Why hadn't I heard it earlier? When everything had seemed completely quiet, it hadn't been completely quiet all the same. That clock . . . and I got angry as I thought about it . . . that huge, tasteless clock had been hanging there pounding the seconds into my head while I'd been sitting there thinking it was quiet, imagining that I couldn't hear a sound. I got the idea that the ticking was actually a continual noise, only interrupted by short pauses. In order to drown it out . . . I don't know . . . I turned the radio on low, but soon regretted it, the music streaming out of it got on my nerves right away, I found. Still, I couldn't bring myself to turn it off now that I'd taken the trouble to turn it on. I caught sight of the newspaper lying on the kitchen counter, which must have been wet, because I could see that water had soaked into the paper and discoloured it. But the front of it was unsullied. And there they were again, those words I'd seen, only in slightly less dramatic letters: *Without Trace.* Then I made up my mind. If a female newsreader comes on the radio at the top of the hour I'll leave her, just pack a suitcase and go, without saying good-bye. But if it's a man I'll go in and lie down quietly beside her, and act like nothing's happened when we wake up in the morning.

I stood completely still, staring at the red hand advancing along its last rotation of the hour. It moved neatly into place on top of the black one . . . for a moment it seemed stuck and unwilling to move on . . . but then it loosened, continuing on into the next hour, without the music dying out or showing any sign of stopping, on the contrary, it rumbled quietly on, as if it had only just gotten started. A minute went by. And then another. And still the music continued. Not without some irritation, I finally had to admit that the kitchen clock was wrong, either it was far too fast or far too slow, and in any case it had made it impossible for me to carry on with my momentous choice. I turned off the music and walked into the dim light of the living room. And as I stared out the window it was as though the low hum of the traffic . . . which I became aware of at the same moment . . . was coming from the narrow gash low down in the sky that had opened up for the first white light of the day.

Foolish, I thought, to imagine you can entrust yourself, your future, to a choice in that way . . . to believe that you can undertake anything at all. Made no less foolish by allowing a crackly transistor radio . . . or in actual fact, I corrected myself, a solitary newsreader working the nightshift on national radio . . . choose for you. The light from the gash . . . which was becoming wider . . . cast a grey tinge over the things in the living room: they looked like they were made of stone, all of them. Solid, immoveable. I walked over to the mantelpiece, the shadow of my head in sharp outline against the wall, like a bust in among all the pictures standing there, the photographs of Helene, and myself, and Marit, and Nina . . . her picture at the very end, and in a different frame, wider and more elaborate than the others. I didn't want to look . . . but forced myself . . . and in a flash it was as though I . . . right before my eyes fell on her face . . . could suddenly remember . . . exactly . . . what she looked like, no, not what she looked like, but what she looks like in that photograph. It's the last photograph that was taken of her, early in June, that summer she should have turned nineteen.

NORWEGIAN LITERATURE SERIES

The Norwegian Literature Series was initiated by the Royal Norwegian Consulate Generals of New York and San Francisco, and the Royal Norwegian Embassy in Washington, D.C., together with NORLA (Norwegian Literature Abroad). Evolving from the relationship begun in 2006 with the publication of Jon Fosse's *Melancholy*, and continued with Stig Sæterbakken's *Siamese* in 2010, this multi-year collaboration with Dalkey Archive Press will enable the publication of major works of Norwegian literature in English translation.

Drawing upon Norway's rich literary tradition, which includes such influential figures as Knut Hamsun and Henrik Ibsen, the Norwegian Literature Series will feature major works from the late modernist period to the present day, from revered figures like Tor Ulven to first novelists like Kjersti A. Skomsvold.

PETROS ABATZOGLOU, *What Does Mrs. Freeman Want?*
MICHAL AJVAZ, *The Golden Age.*
The Other City.
PIERRE ALBERT-BIROT, *Grabinoulor.*
YUZ ALESHKOVSKY, *Kangaroo.*
FELIPE ALFAU, *Chromos.*
Locos.
JOÃO ALMINO, *The Book of Emotions.*
IVAN ÂNGELO, *The Celebration.*
The Tower of Glass.
DAVID ANTIN, *Talking.*
ANTÓNIO LOBO ANTUNES, *Knowledge of Hell.*
The Splendor of Portugal.
ALAIN ARIAS-MISSON, *Theatre of Incest.*
IFTIKHAR ARIF AND WAQAS KHWAJA, EDS., *Modern Poetry of Pakistan.*
JOHN ASHBERY AND JAMES SCHUYLER, *A Nest of Ninnies.*
ROBERT ASHLEY, *Perfect Lives.*
GABRIELA AVIGUR-ROTEM, *Heatwave and Crazy Birds.*
HEIMRAD BÄCKER, *transcript.*
DJUNA BARNES, *Ladies Almanack.*
Ryder.
JOHN BARTH, *LETTERS.*
Sabbatical.
DONALD BARTHELME, *The King.*
Paradise.
SVETISLAV BASARA, *Chinese Letter.*
MIQUEL BAUÇÀ, *The Siege in the Room.*
RENÉ BELLETTO, *Dying.*
MAREK BIEŃCZYK, *Transparency.*
MARK BINELLI, *Sacco and Vanzetti Must Die!*
ANDREI BITOV, *Pushkin House.*
ANDREJ BLATNIK, *You Do Understand.*
LOUIS PAUL BOON, *Chapel Road.*
My Little War.
Summer in Termuren.
ROGER BOYLAN, *Killoyle.*
IGNÁCIO DE LOYOLA BRANDÃO, *Anonymous Celebrity.*
The Good-Bye Angel.
Teeth under the Sun.
Zero.
BONNIE BREMSER, *Troia: Mexican Memoirs.*
CHRISTINE BROOKE-ROSE, *Amalgamemnon.*
BRIGID BROPHY, *In Transit.*
MEREDITH BROSNAN, *Mr. Dynamite.*
GERALD L. BRUNS, *Modern Poetry and the Idea of Language.*
EVGENY BUNIMOVICH AND J. KATES, EDS., *Contemporary Russian Poetry: An Anthology.*
GABRIELLE BURTON, *Heartbreak Hotel.*
MICHEL BUTOR, *Degrees.*
Mobile.
Portrait of the Artist as a Young Ape.
G. CABRERA INFANTE, *Infante's Inferno.*
Three Trapped Tigers.
JULIETA CAMPOS, *The Fear of Losing Eurydice.*
ANNE CARSON, *Eros the Bittersweet.*
ORLY CASTEL-BLOOM, *Dolly City.*
CAMILO JOSÉ CELA, *Christ versus Arizona.*
The Family of Pascual Duarte.
The Hive.
LOUIS-FERDINAND CÉLINE, *Castle to Castle.*
Conversations with Professor Y.
London Bridge.

Normance.
North.
Rigadoon.
MARIE CHAIX, *The Laurels of Lake Constance.*
HUGO CHARTERIS, *The Tide Is Right.*
JEROME CHARYN, *The Tar Baby.*
ERIC CHEVILLARD, *Demolishing Nisard.*
LUIS CHITARRONI, *The No Variations.*
MARC CHOLODENKO, *Mordechai Schamz.*
JOSHUA COHEN, *Witz.*
EMILY HOLMES COLEMAN, *The Shutter of Snow.*
ROBERT COOVER, *A Night at the Movies.*
STANLEY CRAWFORD, *Log of the S.S. The Mrs Unguentine.*
Some Instructions to My Wife.
ROBERT CREELEY, *Collected Prose.*
RENÉ CREVEL, *Putting My Foot in It.*
RALPH CUSACK, *Cadenza.*
SUSAN DAITCH, *L.C.*
Storytown.
NICHOLAS DELBANCO, *The Count of Concord.*
Sherbrookes.
NIGEL DENNIS, *Cards of Identity.*
PETER DIMOCK, *A Short Rhetoric for Leaving the Family.*
ARIEL DORFMAN, *Konfidenz.*
COLEMAN DOWELL,
The Houses of Children.
Island People.
Too Much Flesh and Jabez.
ARKADII DRAGOMOSHCHENKO, *Dust.*
RIKKI DUCORNET, *The Complete Butcher's Tales.*
The Fountains of Neptune.
The Jade Cabinet.
The One Marvelous Thing.
Phosphor in Dreamland.
The Stain.
The Word "Desire."
WILLIAM EASTLAKE, *The Bamboo Bed.*
Castle Keep.
Lyric of the Circle Heart.
JEAN ECHENOZ, *Chopin's Move.*
STANLEY ELKIN, *A Bad Man.*
Boswell: A Modern Comedy.
Criers and Kibitzers, Kibitzers and Criers.
The Dick Gibson Show.
The Franchiser.
George Mills.
The Living End.
The MacGuffin.
The Magic Kingdom.
Mrs. Ted Bliss.
The Rabbi of Lud.
Van Gogh's Room at Arles.
FRANÇOIS EMMANUEL, *Invitation to a Voyage.*
ANNIE ERNAUX, *Cleaned Out.*
SALVADOR ESPRIU, *Ariadne in the Grotesque Labyrinth.*
LAUREN FAIRBANKS, *Muzzle Thyself.*
Sister Carrie.
LESLIE A. FIEDLER, *Love and Death in the American Novel.*
JUAN FILLOY, *Faction.*
Op Oloop.
ANDY FITCH, *Pop Poetics.*
GUSTAVE FLAUBERT, *Bouvard and Pécuchet.*
KASS FLEISHER, *Talking out of School.*

SELECTED DALKEY ARCHIVE TITLES

FORD MADOX FORD,
The March of Literature.
JON FOSSE, *Aliss at the Fire.*
Melancholy.
MAX FRISCH, *I'm Not Stiller.*
Man in the Holocene.
CARLOS FUENTES, *Christopher Unborn.*
Distant Relations.
Terra Nostra.
Vlad.
Where the Air Is Clear.
TAKEHIKO FUKUNAGA, *Flowers of Grass.*
WILLIAM GADDIS, *J R.*
The Recognitions.
JANICE GALLOWAY, *Foreign Parts.*
The Trick Is to Keep Breathing.
WILLIAM H. GASS, *Cartesian Sonata
and Other Novellas.*
Finding a Form.
A Temple of Texts.
The Tunnel.
Willie Masters' Lonesome Wife.
GÉRARD GAVARRY, *Hoppla! 1 2 3.*
Making a Novel.
ETIENNE GILSON,
The Arts of the Beautiful.
Forms and Substances in the Arts.
C. S. GISCOMBE, *Giscome Road.*
Here.
Prairie Style.
DOUGLAS GLOVER, *Bad News of the Heart.*
The Enamoured Knight.
WITOLD GOMBROWICZ,
A Kind of Testament.
PAULO EMÍLIO SALES GOMES, *P's Three
Women.*
KAREN ELIZABETH GORDON, *The Red Shoes.*
GEORGI GOSPODINOV, *Natural Novel.*
JUAN GOYTISOLO, *Count Julian.*
Exiled from Almost Everywhere.
Juan the Landless.
Makbara.
Marks of Identity.
PATRICK GRAINVILLE, *The Cave of Heaven.*
HENRY GREEN, *Back.*
Blindness.
Concluding.
Doting.
Nothing.
JACK GREEN, *Fire the Bastards!*
JIŘÍ GRUŠA, *The Questionnaire.*
GABRIEL GUDDING,
Rhode Island Notebook.
MELA HARTWIG, *Am I a Redundant
Human Being?*
JOHN HAWKES, *The Passion Artist.*
Whistlejacket.
ELIZABETH HEIGHWAY, ED., *Contemporary
Georgian Fiction.*
ALEKSANDAR HEMON, ED.,
Best European Fiction.
AIDAN HIGGINS, *Balcony of Europe.*
A Bestiary.
Blind Man's Bluff
Bornholm Night-Ferry.
Darkling Plain: Texts for the Air.
Flotsam and Jetsam.
Langrishe, Go Down.
Scenes from a Receding Past.
Windy Arbours.
KEIZO HINO, *Isle of Dreams.*
KAZUSHI HOSAKA, *Plainsong.*

ALDOUS HUXLEY, *Antic Hay.*
Crome Yellow.
Point Counter Point.
Those Barren Leaves.
Time Must Have a Stop.
NAOYUKI II, *The Shadow of a Blue Cat.*
MIKHAIL IOSSEL AND JEFF PARKER, EDS.,
*Amerika: Russian Writers View the
United States.*
DRAGO JANČAR, *The Galley Slave.*
GERT JONKE, *The Distant Sound.*
Geometric Regional Novel.
Homage to Czerny.
The System of Vienna.
JACQUES JOUET, *Mountain R.*
Savage.
Upstaged.
CHARLES JULIET, *Conversations with
Samuel Beckett and Bram van
Velde.*
MIEKO KANAI, *The Word Book.*
YORAM KANIUK, *Life on Sandpaper.*
HUGH KENNER, *The Counterfeiters.*
*Flaubert, Joyce and Beckett:
The Stoic Comedians.*
Joyce's Voices.
DANILO KIŠ, *The Attic.*
Garden, Ashes.
The Lute and the Scars
Psalm 44.
A Tomb for Boris Davidovich.
ANITA KONKKA, *A Fool's Paradise.*
GEORGE KONRÁD, *The City Builder.*
TADEUSZ KONWICKI, *A Minor Apocalypse.*
The Polish Complex.
MENIS KOUMANDAREAS, *Koula.*
ELAINE KRAF, *The Princess of 72nd Street.*
JIM KRUSOE, *Iceland.*
AYŞE KULIN, *Farewell: A Mansion in
Occupied Istanbul.*
EWA KURYLUK, *Century 21.*
EMILIO LASCANO TEGUI, *On Elegance
While Sleeping.*
ERIC LAURRENT, *Do Not Touch.*
HERVÉ LE TELLIER, *The Sextine Chapel.*
*A Thousand Pearls (for a Thousand
Pennies)*
VIOLETTE LEDUC, *La Bâtarde.*
EDOUARD LEVÉ, *Autoportrait.*
Suicide.
MARIO LEVI, *Istanbul Was a Fairy Tale.*
SUZANNE JILL LEVINE, *The Subversive
Scribe: Translating Latin
American Fiction.*
DEBORAH LEVY, *Billy and Girl.*
*Pillow Talk in Europe and Other
Places.*
JOSÉ LEZAMA LIMA, *Paradiso.*
ROSA LIKSOM, *Dark Paradise.*
OSMAN LINS, *Avalovara.*
The Queen of the Prisons of Greece.
ALF MAC LOCHLAINN,
The Corpus in the Library.
Out of Focus.
RON LOEWINSOHN, *Magnetic Field(s).*
MINA LOY, *Stories and Essays of Mina Loy.*
BRIAN LYNCH, *The Winner of Sorrow.*
D. KEITH MANO, *Take Five.*
MICHELINE AHARONIAN MARCOM,
The Mirror in the Well.
BEN MARCUS,
The Age of Wire and String.

FOR A FULL LIST OF PUBLICATIONS, VISIT:
www.dalkeyarchive.com

WALLACE MARKFIELD,
  Teitlebaum's Window.
  To an Early Grave.
DAVID MARKSON, *Reader's Block.*
  Springer's Progress.
  Wittgenstein's Mistress.
CAROLE MASO, *AVA.*
LADISLAV MATEJKA AND KRYSTYNA
  POMORSKA, EDS.,
  Readings in Russian Poetics:
    Formalist and Structuralist Views.
HARRY MATHEWS,
  The Case of the Persevering Maltese:
    Collected Essays.
  Cigarettes.
  The Conversions.
  The Human Country: New and
    Collected Stories.
  The Journalist.
  My Life in CIA.
  Singular Pleasures.
  The Sinking of the Odradek
    Stadium.
  Tlooth.
  20 Lines a Day.
JOSEPH MCELROY,
  Night Soul and Other Stories.
THOMAS MCGONIGLE,
  Going to Patchogue.
ROBERT L. MCLAUGHLIN, ED., *Innovations:*
  An Anthology of Modern &
    Contemporary Fiction.
ABDELWAHAB MEDDEB, *Talismano.*
GERHARD MEIER, *Isle of the Dead.*
HERMAN MELVILLE, *The Confidence-Man.*
AMANDA MICHALOPOULOU, *I'd Like.*
STEVEN MILLHAUSER, *The Barnum Museum.*
  In the Penny Arcade.
RALPH J. MILLS, JR., *Essays on Poetry.*
MOMUS, *The Book of Jokes.*
CHRISTINE MONTALBETTI, *The Origin of Man.*
  Western.
OLIVE MOORE, *Spleen.*
NICHOLAS MOSLEY, *Accident.*
  Assassins.
  Catastrophe Practice.
  Children of Darkness and Light.
  Experience and Religion.
  A Garden of Trees.
  God's Hazard.
  The Hesperides Tree.
  Hopeful Monsters.
  Imago Bird.
  Impossible Object.
  Inventing God.
  Judith.
  Look at the Dark.
  Natalie Natalia.
  Paradoxes of Peace.
  Serpent.
  Time at War.
  The Uses of Slime Mould:
    Essays of Four Decades.
WARREN MOTTE,
  Fables of the Novel: French Fiction
    since 1990.
  Fiction Now: The French Novel in
    the 21st Century.
  Oulipo: A Primer of Potential
    Literature.
GERALD MURNANE, *Barley Patch.*
  Inland.

YVES NAVARRE, *Our Share of Time.*
  Sweet Tooth.
DOROTHY NELSON, *In Night's City.*
  Tar and Feathers.
ESHKOL NEVO, *Homesick.*
WILFRIDO D. NOLLEDO, *But for the Lovers.*
FLANN O'BRIEN, *At Swim-Two-Birds.*
  At War.
  The Best of Myles.
  The Dalkey Archive.
  Further Cuttings.
  The Hard Life.
  The Poor Mouth.
  The Third Policeman.
CLAUDE OLLIER, *The Mise-en-Scène.*
  Wert and the Life Without End.
GIOVANNI ORELLI, *Walaschek's Dream.*
PATRIK OUŘEDNÍK, *Europeana.*
  The Opportune Moment, 1855.
BORIS PAHOR, *Necropolis.*
FERNANDO DEL PASO, *News from the Empire.*
  Palinuro of Mexico.
ROBERT PINGET, *The Inquisitory.*
  Mahu or The Material.
  Trio.
A. G. PORTA, *The No World Concerto.*
MANUEL PUIG, *Betrayed by Rita Hayworth.*
  The Buenos Aires Affair.
  Heartbreak Tango.
RAYMOND QUENEAU, *The Last Days.*
  Odile.
  Pierrot Mon Ami.
  Saint Glinglin.
ANN QUIN, *Berg.*
  Passages.
  Three.
  Tripticks.
ISHMAEL REED, *The Free-Lance Pallbearers.*
  The Last Days of Louisiana Red.
  Ishmael Reed: The Plays.
  Juice!
  Reckless Eyeballing.
  The Terrible Threes.
  The Terrible Twos.
  Yellow Back Radio Broke-Down.
JASIA REICHARDT, *15 Journeys Warsaw*
    to London.
NOËLLE REVAZ, *With the Animals.*
JOÃO UBALDO RIBEIRO, *House of the*
    Fortunate Buddhas.
JEAN RICARDOU, *Place Names.*
RAINER MARIA RILKE, *The Notebooks of*
    Malte Laurids Brigge.
JULIÁN RÍOS, *The House of Ulysses.*
  Larva: A Midsummer Night's Babel.
  Poundemonium.
  Procession of Shadows.
AUGUSTO ROA BASTOS, *I the Supreme.*
DANIËL ROBBERECHTS, *Arriving in Avignon.*
JEAN ROLIN, *The Explosion of the*
    Radiator Hose.
OLIVIER ROLIN, *Hotel Crystal.*
ALIX CLEO ROUBAUD, *Alix's Journal.*
JACQUES ROUBAUD, *The Form of a*
    City Changes Faster, Alas, Than
    the Human Heart.
  The Great Fire of London.
  Hortense in Exile.
  Hortense Is Abducted.
  The Loop.
  Mathematics:
    The Plurality of Worlds of Lewis.

FOR A FULL LIST OF PUBLICATIONS, VISIT:
www.dalkeyarchive.com